It's our

Mary-Kate and Ashley

Sweet 16

Win two fragrances
from the *mary-kateandashley*
brand!
Details on page 131.

Mary-Kate and Ashley
Sweet 16

All That Glitters

By Eliza Willard

HarperEntertainment

An Imprint of HarperCollins*Publishers*

A PARACHUTE PRESS BOOK

A PARACHUTE PRESS BOOK

Parachute Publishing, L.L.C.
156 Fifth Avenue, Suite 302
New York, NY 10010

Published by
HarperEntertainment
An Imprint of HarperCollins*Publishers*
10 East 53rd Street, New York, NY 10022-5299

SWEET 16 books are created and produced by Parachute Press, L.L.C., in cooperation with Dualstar Publications, a division of Dualstar Entertainment Group, LLC., published by HarperEntertainment, an imprint of HarperCollins Publishers.

ISBN 0-06-055646-3

HarperCollins®, █®, and HarperEntertainment™ are trademarks of HarperCollins Publishers Inc.

First printing: June 2003

Printed in the United States of America

Visit HarperEntertainment on the World Wide Web at
www.harpercollins.com

10 9 8 7 6 5 4 3 2 1

chapter one

"David, where are you going?" I asked. My handsome boyfriend trained his steely blue eyes on me.

"None of your business," he rasped in a voice I hardly recognized.

What had happened to him? Why was he acting like this? He started toward the door. I ran to him, clutching his sleeve. "David, what's wrong with you? Please tell me!" I begged.

"You don't want to know," he said.

"But I do!" I cried. "I don't care how bad it is. I love you!"

David's mouth cracked into a slow grin. "You fool," he muttered through his teeth. "Haven't you figured it out yet?"

"What? Figured out what?" I asked.

He slowly unwound his red scarf from around

his neck. The red scarf he always wore. The scarf I gave him for Christmas . . .

"I'm the Disco Strangler," he said, snapping the scarf in his hands.

"No!" I screamed, backing toward the door. "No, it can't be true. . . !"

"Psst! Mikki!"

I turned around. It took me a few seconds to remember where I was.

"Hey, Mikki!" Danielle whispered. "Come back to us, Mikki!"

My friends Danielle Bloom and Tyler McGuire waved to me from behind a big camera crane. Danielle giggled. My face turned red.

I wasn't facing down my killer boyfriend in a San Francisco apartment. I was on a movie set in Vancouver. On the set of *Killer Boyfriend*, to be exact. And I was watching two big movie stars— Danielle's mom, Diana Donovan, and Tyler's dad, Kyle McGuire—act out the scene.

But I got so caught up in it, I found myself mouthing the words along with Diana. I'd watched her rehearse the scene for two hours the night before, so I had it memorized.

"Come over here, Mikki," Danielle whispered.

I walked away from the soundstage quietly, so I wouldn't disturb the scene. Mikki was my new nickname. Diana Donovan made it up. She started out calling me M.K., short for Mary-Kate. But soon it changed to Mikki. I thought it was cute. And anyway, who was I to argue with an Oscar-winning actress? If she wanted to call me Mikki, I wasn't going to stop her. I couldn't wait to see what my sister, Ashley, thought of it when I got home.

"What's up, Mikster?" Tyler said.

"You should have seen your face!" Danielle said to me.

She has strawberry-blond hair, and her pretty green eyes lit up as she laughed at me.

She added, "You looked like you were really afraid Kyle was going to strangle you!"

"That's the sign of a great actress," Tyler said. "She got into the character so much, she thought the scene was real."

"Thanks," I said, but I still felt embarrassed.

"Hey, I know a natural when I see one," Tyler said.

Tyler's father, Kyle McGuire, was a heartthrob in the 1970s. Now Tyler, at seventeen, was even cuter than his dad. They had the same flinty blue eyes and straight blue-black hair. Tyler's mom was a beautiful model, and he had inherited her long eyelashes and fine bones. Kyle's face was chiseled and tough, while Tyler's was more delicate.

"Cut!" Steven Peterman, the director, called out. All around us the cast and crew relaxed. "Diana, I like the terror you're giving me, but I need more of it. Remember, your whole world just turned upside down. Let's try it again."

"This is boring," Danielle said. "Let's get out of here."

"They've got fresh doughnuts at catering," Tyler suggested.

"I'm there," I said.

We headed outside to the catering truck. Catering supplied food for everybody on the set during filming and had pretty much anything anyone wanted to eat. We grabbed some doughnuts and coffee and headed for a picnic table in the shade. The blue harbor shimmered in the distance. Summer in Vancouver is pretty sweet.

I was amazed when Diana invited me to go on location to keep Danielle company for two weeks—amazed and a little nervous. Danielle and I met when we starred together in our school's production of *Grease*. We weren't too crazy about each other at first.

In the beginning Danielle refused to be in a school play—Diana was very critical of her acting, and Danielle couldn't deal with it. But Diana thought it would be good for Danielle, and I convinced her to do it—eventually. I guess Diana was grateful to me for that. Anyway, she always seemed to like me.

We watched the boats in the harbor as we munched our doughnuts and sipped our coffee.

"Have you guys seen *Interplay* yet?" Tyler asked. "It's brilliant." *Interplay* was the latest movie by Lars Hansen, a famous Swedish director.

"Diana dragged me to a screening of it at the studio," Danielle said.

Danielle always called her mother by her first name. I thought it was very sophisticated. Her parents are divorced, and Danielle uses her dad's last name.

"She loves Hansen because he's so good with actors," Danielle added. "She always says she'd give anything to be in one of his movies."

I didn't know what to say. I hadn't seen *Interplay*. I hadn't seen any Lars Hansen movies. Well, I think I saw one on TV late one night. It was in black and white, in Swedish, with subtitles. A man and a woman kept hitting a tennis ball back and forth, back and forth, over and over again. The whole time they kept talking about strawberries.

"Soon the strawberries will be ripe," the woman would say. Then the man would respond, "Yes, the summer brings the strawberries."

Finally, Ashley grabbed the remote from me and turned to a *Spencer Academy* rerun.

"What about you, Mikki?" Tyler asked. "What's the last movie you saw?"

"*One Plus One*," I admitted a little sheepishly.

One Plus One was a fluffy romantic comedy—not in the same league as a serious Swedish film.

"I haven't seen that yet," Danielle said. "Did you like it?"

I wasn't sure what to say. There wasn't much to the movie. "It was cute."

Tyler nodded. "I liked it. It reminded me of those old screwball comedies from the thirties. I thought it had real texture to it. You know? It was really layered."

He looked at me, waiting for me to agree or disagree. The problem was, I had no idea what he was talking about.

But he was obviously expecting an answer, so I had to say something. "Yeah, the layering was amazing," I said. "I couldn't get enough of that texture."

"I'll have to go see it, then," Danielle said. "I was going to skip it because I can't stand Amanda Wilkinson." Amanda Wilkinson was the star of *One Plus One*.

She continued, "She did *Brave Girls* with Diana and was a total diva. And she wasn't even famous yet."

I secretly pinched my leg under the table. I couldn't believe I was talking insider gossip with the kids of two stars! It was beyond exciting. I couldn't add much to the conversation, but just listening was fun.

"Hey, Amanda's cool," Tyler said.

"You just think she's hot," Danielle shot back.

"That's not true!" Tyler said. "I mean, she *is* hot. But she used to baby-sit for my little sisters, and they loved her."

"You have sisters?" I asked Tyler. "How old are they?"

"Daisy is six and Emma is eight," he said. "They're really cute. Bratty, but cute. They're back in New York with my mother. How about you? Any brothers or sisters?"

"I've got a twin sister, Ashley," I told him. "I miss her, even though I've been away for only a couple of weeks. We've never spent much time apart."

"I wish I had a brother or sister," Danielle said. "Then maybe Diana would give me a break once in a while."

There was an uncomfortable silence. Diana was ambitious, and she pushed Danielle pretty hard. She wanted Danielle to be a great actress, as successful as she was or maybe even more. The trouble was, how could you be more successful than Diana?

"I wanted to be an actor when I was younger, but Dad talked me out of it," Tyler confided. "He says it's too unpredictable. But I love movies. After I graduate next year I'm going to film school. I want to be a director."

"You'd be great at that," I said. He knew so much about movies.

"I want to be an actress," Danielle said. "But Diana's trying to turn me into a clone of herself."

"But she's a great actress and so beautiful," I said. "Who wouldn't want to be like her?"

Danielle made a face.

Tyler glanced at his watch. "Whoa, it's after six," he said. "I've got to go back to Dad's trailer. I promised Daisy and Emma I'd call them as soon as they got home from school. See you two later."

He hurried off toward the trailers. He was so cute—and so nice. It was too bad he lived in New

York and I lived in Malibu. So far away . . .

I sighed. "I wonder if I'll ever get to see Tyler again after this."

Danielle tossed her half-eaten doughnut in the trash. "You might as well forget it," she said. "A gorgeous guy like that has *got* to have a girlfriend at home."

"He hasn't said anything about a girlfriend," I protested.

"So? Why should he?" Danielle said. "This way he can flirt with all the girls on the set."

"He's not really a flirt," I said. "He's serious and kind of thoughtful."

"Whatever," Danielle said. "I'm chilly. Let's go back to the trailer."

We walked to Diana's trailer as the sun began to set. We went inside and flicked on a light. *This is so cool,* I thought for about the hundredth time as I looked around.

Diana's trailer was fancier than most people's houses. It had a living room, a kitchen, and a small bedroom, all decorated in various shades of cream. Cream-colored walls, comfy cream-colored couches and chairs, tables, refrigerator, bed, carpet—everything. And the most amazing thing was, every time Diana made a movie, she got another trailer exactly like this—right down to the cream-colored dishes and the white lilies on the coffee table.

"It's in her contract," Danielle had told me.

Before Diana agreed to do a movie, her manager gave the studio a list of special conditions that had to be met, including the way the trailer was decorated and the individually packaged salads—mesclun greens with dried cranberries and balsamic vinaigrette—that filled the fridge.

Danielle opened the fridge and handed me a salad, a fork, and a bottle of spring water. We settled on the overstuffed couch.

"Ugh," she groaned as she opened the salad container. "Doesn't Diana ever get sick of this stuff?"

I'd never get sick of it, I thought, digging into my salad. But I didn't say anything.

The door opened and Diana breezed in, followed by her personal assistant, Miranda. Diana's normally red hair had been dyed blond for the movie. Everyone said it was almost the exact same shade as mine.

"Don't forget to have the dry cleaning delivered tomorrow, darling," Diana said. She wore her big dark sunglasses all the time—even at night and even indoors.

Miranda, a tall, skinny woman in her late

twenties with brown bangs and glasses, nodded and took notes.

"And call Morty back to reschedule that meeting," Diana added. "I won't be up to seeing him my first day back in Los Angeles."

Miranda nodded again and scribbled. Her cell phone rang. She answered it and moved toward the bedroom to take the call.

"That's not Lola, is it?" Diana asked Miranda. Lola was Diana's yoga teacher. Miranda shook her head. "It's for me," she told Diana.

"Let me know if Lola calls, please, love," Diana said. Then she perched on a big stuffed chair, whipped off her sunglasses, and smiled at Danielle and me. "Hello, darlings. Did you have a good time today?"

Danielle rolled her eyes and didn't answer.

I said, "I learned so much just from watching you on the set today, Diana. You were amazing!"

Diana smiled and glanced at Danielle. "Thank you, Mikki darling. I'm glad you're keeping your eyes open. There are a lot of talented people working on this production."

"I'm learning so much about everything!" I said. "I'm having the best time!"

Diana laughed. "I wish Danielle was as enthusiastic as you are."

11

Danielle plunked her salad container on the coffee table. "Diana, what do you expect? You've been dragging me from location to location since I was five. By now I've learned just about everything there is to know. There's not all that much to it, believe me."

Diana frowned. I froze, my fork halfway to my mouth. I hated these tense moments between them, and they happened so often. I liked Danielle a lot. But why couldn't she see how lucky she was?

There was a knock on the door. Miranda answered it and Steven Peterman stepped in.

"Hi, girls. Good work today, Diana," he said. "The producers just called from Los Angeles. They said the buzz about this film is phenomenal down there. People are already talking Oscar!"

"That's wonderful, darling!" Diana said.

"They're going to want you and Kyle to do some preliminary publicity as soon as you get back to Los Angeles," Steven told her. "Not too much, just a few interviews."

"Fine, love," Diana said.

"About tomorrow's scene," Steven went on. "It's our last day of shooting, so we've got to make it count. The scene is very short, but it's crucial. You're at a party and you see David across the room. . . ."

Danielle picked up a teen magazine from the coffee table. "Look at this, Mikki," she said, reading the cover. "'Take our exclusive personality quiz. What type are you?'"

"Uh-huh," I said, but I was straining to hear the conversation between Steven and Diana at the same time. I wanted to soak up as much as I could for the short time I was on the set.

"Let's take it," Danielle said. She opened the magazine. "Question one: 'Are you an early riser or a late sleeper?'"

"Why is your character drawn to David?" Steven was saying. "What's her motivation? What's missing in her life at that moment? That's what I need to see from you. . . ."

"Mikki," Danielle said. "Answer the question!"

"Um, okay," I said. I wished Danielle was more interested in her mother's career. It was hard to learn much when she was always distracting me. "I'm a late sleeper."

"Me, too," Danielle said, checking off a box in the magazine. "Okay, 'which do you like better, sweet things or salty?'"

"Sweet," I answered, trying to hear what Diana and Steven were saying to each other. I caught a few scraps.

"The party scene will fade away," Steven said, "and the color of the walls will change. They'll throb like a beating heart, changing color with each beat—"

"—and the colors will represent how she feels," Diana cut in.

"Exactly," Steven said. "Behind you we'll see a lonely blue, a romantic pink . . . And behind him maybe a sharp, greedy green . . ."

"'Which of these animals would you prefer as a pet?'" Danielle went on. "'A. Dog. B. Cat. C. Rabbit. Or D. Monkey.'"

"Um—" I wished Danielle would just stop for a minute. How many chances did I get to listen in on a conversation between one of the most famous directors and one of the most famous actresses in the world? We could do the quiz anytime.

"I'm going to say cat," Danielle said. "Mikki?"

"Monkey," I replied.

A few minutes later Steven got ready to leave. He waved to me and Danielle. "See you girls at the cast party tomorrow night?"

I glanced at Diana, who smiled and nodded. "It's cast only, but I think we can make an exception for you two," she said.

"It wouldn't be a party without these lovely

young ladies," Steven added. He opened the trailer door and stepped outside. "Bright and early tomorrow, Diana."

"Don't worry, darling, I'll be there," she promised.

"I didn't know there was a cast party tomorrow night!" I said. I tried not to show how excited I was. Danielle seemed bored by the idea, as usual. "What are you going to wear?"

"I don't know," Danielle said. "It's always the same old people at those things."

The same old people? She was talking about Kyle McGuire! And Tyler, of course.

My mind raced. Tomorrow night was going to be the most exciting night of my life!

chapter two

"Sushi?" the waitress asked, offering me a tray of colorful raw fish on rice.

"Thank you," I said. I picked up a piece of bright red tuna. It melted in my mouth as I looked around the room.

The producers had rented out the trendiest restaurant in Vancouver for the wrap party of *Killer Boyfriend*. The crowd looked beautiful. The men were slouchy and casual in jeans and designer shirts. The women were dressier, mostly wearing high-heeled sandals and clingy, colorful dresses.

I glanced down at my sleeveless pink dress and hoped I looked all right. Danielle had loaned me some long turquoise earrings to go with it. I fit in pretty well, I thought.

I scanned the crowd as a song from one of my

favorite bands, Rave, played on the sound system. Diana stood near the bar with Steven, greeting everyone with kisses on both cheeks. I didn't see Tyler.

"Mikki, do you know Cleo Raymond?" Danielle led me to a tall, pretty brunette standing beside a shorter guy with wholesome frat-boy good looks. "And this is Colin Davies."

"Hi," I said. "We met on the set."

Cleo and Colin are both up-and-coming actors in their early twenties with supporting roles in *Killer Boyfriend*. Rumor had it they'd started an on-set romance but were trying to keep it secret. I caught Colin just barely tickling Cleo's hand.

"Ugh, I wish they'd take off this stupid music," Cleo complained. "I liked Rave when I was about twelve."

"The D.J.s in Vancouver are at least a year behind us," Colin added. "I went to five clubs while we were here and didn't dance once."

"We went out dancing one night," I said. Diana had taken me and Danielle to a club our second night in Vancouver. "A guy from the Wild Palms was there." The Wild Palms was a Canadian band Ashley and I were really getting into.

"Oh, yeah, the Wild Palms," Cleo said. "They're

so . . . Top Forty. You don't really like them, do you?"

"Uh—no," I lied. I didn't want to look uncool. "My sister likes them," I added, trying to cover up. "She's all over that Top Forty stuff."

"What did you guys do last night?" Danielle asked.

"What *could* we do?" Colin replied. "We hit all the clubs. There's nothing left but *bowling*."

"I love bowling," I blurted out. "I have my own bowling ball at home."

Cleo, Colin, and Danielle stared at me.

"You do?" Colin asked.

"Of course she does," Danielle said, coming to my rescue. "Collecting dust in her closet. Bowling was a big craze when we were in junior high."

"That makes sense," Cleo said. "Bowling is so three-years-ago."

A waiter swooped past us. "Excuse me," he said. "Dinner will be served in a few minutes. Please take your seats."

Danielle and I wove through the crowd toward the head table, where Diana, Steven, Kyle, and Tyler were already seated.

"It's the Mikster," Tyler said when he saw me. "Grab a chair." He patted the seat between himself and Diana. I sat down. Danielle sat on his other side.

Another waiter stopped at our table. "Can I get you all something to drink?" he asked.

"Darling, bring me an iced green tea with a splash of peach nectar, please," Diana ordered. "And a lemon on the side."

"Me, too," Danielle said.

I really wanted a diet soda, but I decided to follow the crowd. "I'll have the same, please," I ordered.

"Ginger ale for me," Tyler said.

"So, Tyler, are you going back to New York tomorrow?" I asked.

He nodded. "It's a long flight. Good thing I'm flying first class."

"I know what you mean," I said.

Diana had flown me and Danielle to Vancouver first class. It was amazing. We each had our own personal TV screen so that we could watch movies or whatever we wanted. And the food actually tasted okay.

"They're having a heat wave in New York," Tyler told me. "Daisy said all the candles on our terrace melted. That's going to be hard to get used to after a week here in cool Vancouver."

"Los Angeles is always the same," I said. "Not too hot, not too cold. Sometimes I wonder what it would be like to live in a place that has four seasons."

"Come visit me in New York sometime and you'll see," Tyler offered. "You'll love it! The leaves turning red, slogging through the dirty slush, getting splashed by taxis that won't pick you up in the pouring rain . . ."

I laughed, but I secretly wished I *could* visit Tyler in New York, dirty slush and all.

Diana tapped me on the arm. "Mikki darling, I just want to tell you how glad I am that you came along on location with us. You and Danielle have gotten to be good friends, haven't you?"

"Yes, we have," I answered.

"She needs a good friend like you," Diana said. "Listen, when we get back to Los Angeles, don't be a stranger. You have an open invitation to come to our house anytime."

Wow! An open invitation to Diana Donovan's house!

"Thank you," I said.

"I'll be very busy with publicity and post-production for this film," Diana said. "Maybe you could keep Danielle company."

"I'd love to," I said. "What happens in post-production?"

"Oh, you know, editing, looping, overdubbing, sound effects, music . . . It's usually a bore, but you might find it interesting if you've never seen it before. You and Danielle are welcome to tag along."

"That would be fantastic!" I said.

"Fabulous," Diana said. She turned away to talk to Steven.

I was so excited, I could feel myself glowing. These past two weeks on the set had been so exciting—and now I knew it didn't have to end. I'd learn even more once we got home!

After dinner, people started dancing. Danielle and I went to the bar for more iced green tea with peach nectar.

"We're not leaving with you tomorrow after all," Danielle told me. "Turns out Diana has to stay in Vancouver an extra day."

"That's all right," I said. "I'll see you when you get home."

"Seriously, you've got to come over for dinner our first night back," Danielle said. "You know how things get between me and Diana sometimes. Especially when it's just the two of us. But Diana likes you, and she doesn't criticize me as much when you're around. So will you come?"

"Don't worry, I'll be there," I said.

"Good," Danielle said. "It's been so great having you on the set. It takes some of the pressure off me. Being home alone with Diana again will take some getting used to."

"I don't mind at all," I said. "I like spending time with you guys."

We settled back down at our table. Tyler pulled something out of his jacket pocket. "Here, Mikki—I brought this for you," he said, handing me a book. "It's one of my favorites."

"*Directors on Directing,*" I read. "'The world's great directors discuss film and theater technique.' Wow, Tyler, that's so thoughtful of you. Thank you."

"It's an excellent book," Tyler said. "I thought you'd like it."

"I'll read it on the plane home," I promised. I opened the front cover. On the title page, Tyler had written his E-mail address.

"I want to stay in touch," he explained. "I figured we could E-mail each other once in a while. Is that cool?"

"Of course," I said. "I'd like that."

Inside I was bursting. I'd never gotten a present like this from a guy before.

A Rave song came on over the sound system. "Want to dance?" Tyler asked. "I love this song."

"Me, too," I agreed, glad that Tyler still liked Rave, even if Cleo thought they were uncool.

Here I am at a wrap party, dancing with a movie star's son, I thought.

How can I ever go back to my normal life?

chapter three

"Do you see her, Ashley?" Mom asked as we watched people pour off a flight from Vancouver.

"Not yet," I said. I stood on tiptoe in the Los Angeles airport, straining to get a glimpse of Mary-Kate. She'd been away for two whole weeks and I really missed her. I fingered the gold locket at my throat. Wait until she heard all the news!

At last I spotted a blond girl wearing big, dark sunglasses and a pale pink scarf tied over her head.

"Is that her?" I asked, pointing.

Mom and Dad stared at the girl.

"It sure looks like her," Dad said. "But why is she wearing her scarf that way?"

"She's just trying out a new style," Mom said. "It's definitely Mary-Kate."

Mom, Dad, and I all waved to her until she

looked up and noticed us. She grinned and ran over to hug us.

"Welcome home, honey!" Dad said, squeezing her.

"Did you have a good time?" Mom asked.

"I had a fantastic time, darlings!" Mary-Kate said, kissing all of us on both cheeks.

Darlings? I thought. *What was up with that?*

"Aren't you going to take off your sunglasses, honey?" Mom asked her.

"Oh! I didn't even realize I had them on," Mary-Kate said. She pulled off her sunglasses and blinked in the light.

"I'm so glad you're back, Mary-Kate!" I said, hugging her one more time.

A funny look crossed Mary-Kate's face for a split second—as if she'd just eaten a lemon.

"It's good to be home," she said, smiling again. "But I have a teensy favor to ask."

Dad picked up her carry-on bag, and we headed for the baggage claim.

"Ask away," Mom said.

"Well, I don't want to be Mary-Kate anymore," Mary-Kate said. "I'd like you to call me Mikki."

Mikki? "Where did that come from?" I asked.

"Diana started it while we were on the set,"

Mary-Kate said, "and it just caught on. I really like it. So—would you guys mind calling me Mikki from now on?"

I glanced at Mom and Dad.

Dad shrugged and said, "Whatever you want, Mary-Ka—I mean, Mikki."

"Thanks, guys." Mary-Kate grinned. I didn't care what she wanted us to call her—I was just glad she was back!

And anyway, I was sure she didn't really expect me, her twin sister, to call her something new after all these years. Diana Donovan could call her whatever she wanted. To me she just wasn't a "Mikki."

We picked up Mary-Kate's luggage and stopped at Big Jonesy's Diner on the way home to celebrate her return. Mary-Kate put her sunglasses back on in the car and didn't take them off again—not even in the restaurant.

We both loved Big Jonesy's. It was a cute 1950s-style diner loaded with shiny chrome and aqua trim. Mom and Dad had been taking us to Jonesy's since we were little.

A waitress dressed in an aqua uniform and a towering fire-engine-red beehive hairdo stopped at our table. "All right, hon, what'll you have?" she asked me.

"I'll have a cola float with cherry ice cream," I said, "and she'll have a vanilla root beer float." I nodded toward Mary-Kate. Mary-Kate *always* orders a vanilla root beer float at Jonesy's.

But Mary-Kate shook her head. "No—scratch that," she told the waitress. "I'd like iced green tea with a splash of peach nectar, lemon on the side, please."

What? I stared at her. The waitress stared at her. Mom and Dad were speechless.

"You want *what*, now?" the waitress asked.

"Iced green tea—" Mary-Kate began.

"We haven't got green tea," the waitress said. "Not to mention peach nectar. So pick something else."

"Just sparkling water with lime, then, please," Mary-Kate ordered.

"One seltzer," the waitress said.

"You're not getting a float?" I asked.

Mary-Kate shrugged. "I've grown out of that, I guess."

Weird, I thought.

"Iced green tea," Dad said. "Somebody's getting fancy."

"It's perfectly normal," Mary-Kate insisted. "Any *real* restaurant would have it."

"So tell us all about your trip," Mom said. "Don't you want to take off your sunglasses, Mary-Kate?"

Mary-Kate cleared her throat. "Mikki," she corrected Mom. "I'm more comfortable this way."

Mom suppressed a grin. "Sorry, *Mikki*. Did you get to watch Diana film her scenes?"

"Every day," Mary-Kate said. "I learned so much! I watched all the actors and the director and even the camera crew. I learned about acting technique and camera angles and different kinds of shots. . . ."

She was talking fast because she was excited.

"It was so cool!" she continued. "One night Diana took me and Danielle out to a restaurant. We heard all this noise outside as we were getting ready to leave. Turns out some photographers spotted Diana. They were waiting for us at the entrance! So we sneaked through the kitchen and left by the back door. The photographers never caught on. It was hilarious!"

"I guess Danielle is used to that," Mom said.

"Totally," Mary-Kate said. "But for me it was weird. All these bright lights flashing in your eyes! It's kind of scary. But exciting, too."

"What were the other actors like?" I asked.

She grinned at me, and I could tell she was thinking about a boy. Call it sisterly intuition.

"Kyle McGuire was great—he brought his son, Tyler, to the set," Mary-Kate told me.

"And—?" I asked.

"He's seventeen and so cute!" Mary-Kate gushed. "He lives in New York, so we're going to E-mail."

"Excellent," I said.

"Oh, and Diana asked me if I wanted to hang out with her and Steven during post-production here in Los Angeles," she added to Mom and Dad. "Is that okay?"

"Who's Steven?" Dad asked.

"Steven Peterman, the director," Mary-Kate replied.

Mom and Dad looked at each other. "Sounds fine to me," Mom said.

"You'll really learn a lot," Dad said. "Post-production is the most important part of some movies."

I squirmed as I listened to Mary-Kate's stories. I loved hearing all about her trip—but I was bursting with news, too! Finally Mary-Kate paused for a breath, and I jumped in.

"Guess what?" I told her. "Lucas learned to

crawl! I was there when he did it for the first time!"

Lucas is our friend Brittany Bowen's baby brother. We'd all spent so much time baby-sitting for him we felt as if we were his big sisters, too.

"That's fantastic!" Mary-Kate said. "I can't wait to see him."

"And Ben bought a car!" I added. Ben Jones is our friend Lauren Glazer's boyfriend. He'd been working two jobs after school, saving all his money—and it finally paid off.

"What kind?" Mary-Kate asked.

"A Honda," I told her. "Used, but still—it's pretty cool. It has a sunroof. Lauren is so excited."

I fingered the gold locket around my neck. I'd saved the best news for last.

"Excellent," Mary-Kate said. "And what about Aaron? How was your anniversary?"

She remembered! My boyfriend, Aaron Moore, and I had just celebrated our two-month anniversary. That was part of the great news.

"It was wonderful!" I told her. "He took me bowling."

That same lemon-eating look crossed Mary-Kate's face. But why? She loves bowling. Anyway, it passed, so I ignored it.

"And right after the tenth frame," I finished, "he

gave me this." I pulled the locket out from under my sweater and showed it to Mary-Kate.

"It's beautiful!" She gasped.

"And look!" I said, opening the locket. "He put our pictures inside it!"

Mary-Kate smiled as she peered at the tiny photos of me and Aaron. "It's so sweet," she said. "Did I show you what Tyler gave me?"

She reached into her bag and pulled out a paperback book, *Directors on Directing*.

"He's going to film school after he graduates from prep school next year," Mary-Kate said. "I think he's going to be a great director someday! You wouldn't believe how brilliant he is when he talks about movies. He's so . . . so—insightful!"

"Wait, uh, Mikki," Mom said, obviously struggling with Mary-Kate's new nickname. "Ashley still hasn't told you the biggest news of all."

"What?" Mary-Kate put her book away.

"The Sunshine Day Care Center is finally reopening!" Mom announced.

Mom runs the day-care center, and she'd been working on expanding and remodeling it for months.

Mom continued, "And we're having a big grand-opening celebration!"

"With a play and everything!" I added.

"A play?" Mary-Kate said.

"Your sister volunteered to direct a production of *Snow White and the Seven Dwarfs*," Dad told her. "Starring some of your friends and a lot of adorable four-year-olds from the center."

"We've built a beautiful new auditorium and we want to show it off," Mom said.

"Lauren is playing Snow White," I said. "Ben will play the prince, and Aaron is the hunter. Brittany is making the sets. The kids are playing the dwarfs and other small parts like trees, bears, rabbits, raccoons. . . . And I saved the best part of all for you, Mikki"—I managed to spit out the nickname without stumbling too much—"the Wicked Queen!"

"That sounds fabulous!" Mary-Kate said. "Can I be your assistant director? I learned so much from being on the set with Diana. It would be cool to have a chance to use it."

"Great," I said. "You can teach me your new techniques. Our next rehearsal is Tuesday afternoon. Everyone will be there."

"Good," Mary-Kate said. "I can't wait to see Brittany and Lauren and everybody."

"You'll see them sooner than you think," I said.

I had another surprise for her that I was very excited about. "I invited all our friends over to hang by the pool tomorrow night. We can swim, eat a little Mexican food . . ."

"Tomorrow night?" Mary-Kate frowned. "I'm busy tomorrow night."

"You are?" I couldn't believe it. She already had plans? "What are you doing?"

"I promised Danielle I'd go to her house for dinner," she said. "She and Diana are getting back tomorrow, and they haven't been getting along so well lately—"

"But you just spent two whole weeks with Danielle!" I protested. "And you haven't seen your friends in ages!"

"I know," Mary-Kate said. "But I promised Danielle."

"Can't you have dinner with her the next night?" I asked. "Everybody's looking forward to seeing you."

"I'm sorry," Mary-Kate said. "I wish I'd known about it sooner. But Danielle's counting on me."

"I'm sure Danielle will understand," Mom said. "Ashley planned such a nice little get-together for you, Mary-Kate."

"Mom, I'd really appreciate it if you'd call me Mikki from now on," Mary-Kate said. "Okay?"

I stared at my sister. I didn't know what to think. The scarf, the sunglasses, the iced green tea, the kisses on both cheeks and—worst of all—Mikki. It was all too much for me. What was going on with her? She was gone for only two weeks. How could someone change so much so quickly?

chapter four

"**W**ow, I *love* this dress." I gasped.

Danielle looked over at me. "Which one, Mikki?"

I pulled the dress out of Danielle's closet and held it up in front of me. I fingered the gold sequins on the fluffy ballerina skirt. "Where did you wear this one?" I asked.

"To the *Dark Horses* opening," Danielle said. "Diana wasn't in it, but she wanted to go to the opening because she knew there'd be a lot of press there."

I was in Danielle's room, looking at all the beautiful clothes in her huge walk-in closet. The closet was almost as big as my whole bedroom. Everything was organized by style and color, with matching shoes on a rack underneath. It was the most incredible closet I had ever seen. But I had a feeling Diana's was even more impressive.

"This whole row is outfits for movie openings." Danielle waved her hand over a rack of sparkling dresses. "I have to be careful never to wear the same dress to two events. The press might notice—and they can be brutal. Remember when Luciana Albini wore the same dress twice in a month? The tabloids ripped her to shreds!"

I did remember seeing photos of the Italian movie star at two different parties in the same outfit. The headline read: "She Makes $1 Million a Picture and Can't Afford a New Dress!"

"They're just so beautiful," I said, admiring a pink satin gown.

"You can borrow them anytime you want, Mikki," Danielle offered. "I can't wear them, but someone should."

"Wow! Thank you!" I said.

I draped the pink dress in front of me and checked myself out in the mirror. Where would I ever wear such stunning clothes? To go out for pizza? A school dance? Forget it! My life just wasn't that glamorous. Still, Danielle was generous to offer them to me.

She yanked a jacket off a hanger and tossed it

to me. "Try that on," she said. "It'll look great on you."

It was a black satin jacket with white trim. On the back, in red letters, was the logo for *Brave Girls*, the movie Diana had starred in with Amanda Wilkinson. It was the kind of jacket only the cast and crew get to wear while they're working on a film.

I slipped the jacket on and looked in the mirror. "This is so cool," I said.

"Keep it," Danielle offered. "I've got another one."

"Thanks, Danielle," I said.

There was a gentle knock at the door. "Excuse me, Danielle." It was Diana's maid, Estelle. "Dinner is ready."

"Great, I'm starving," Danielle said.

We left her beautiful room, with its white carpet and its own terrace overlooking the pool, and headed downstairs to the small dining area off the living room. The house had a big dining room for formal parties, a breakfast nook in the kitchen, and this more casual eating area near the fireplace.

"Mikki darling, I'm so glad you could join us for dinner tonight," Diana said. She was dressed in jeans and a sweater, but somehow on her they looked elegant and chic.

"Thank you for having me," I said.

I sat down, and Estelle filled our water glasses.

"Post-production starts in a few days," Diana told me while Estelle served the dinner.

We had salad, broiled fish with a delicious sauce, and wild rice with pine nuts and cranberries. Diana is really into cranberries.

I could be home eating gloppy tacos and refried beans, I thought—and I didn't miss them one bit.

"Steven agreed to let you watch the film editor at work if you'd like," Diana went on. "That's always fun—you'll see whose lines end up on the cutting-room floor!"

She laughed, and I laughed along with her, even though I didn't really see what was so funny.

"After they finish editing, I'll have to go in for looping," Diana went on. "That's in case a few of my lines can't be heard clearly, or there's some other problem. I just say the lines over again, timing it to the picture."

"That sounds fascinating," I said. "I'd love to see how that works."

"Would you, darling?" Diana said. "Well, why don't you come along?"

"I'd love to!" I said.

"Huh." Danielle snorted. "You never asked me if

I wanted to sit in on looping." She stabbed a piece of lettuce on her fork.

"*Would* you like to go, Danielle?" Diana asked. "I didn't know you were interested, love."

"Yes! It'll be fun!" I added.

Danielle scowled. "I'd rather eat lint."

Diana looked away. "Well," she said. "I'm glad I asked."

The table was uncomfortably silent for a few minutes. My fork clicked against the china as I ate. Danielle and Diana pushed their food around on their plates.

Diana suddenly brightened up. "Mikki darling, what's been going on at your house since you got home? I'll bet your family was glad to see you."

"Yes—" I began. I thought a little guiltily of Ashley and all my friends hanging out by the pool at our house that very moment—without me.

But Danielle cut in, "Mikki's putting on a kiddie play at a day-care center."

My face reddened a little. Why did Danielle have to bring that up? It was so small-time compared to Diana's career. I felt embarrassed.

"Oh? How lovely! What play?" Diana asked.

I would have liked to name one of Shakespeare's plays, but I knew I should tell the truth.

"*Snow White and the Seven Dwarfs*," I said. I took a bite of my fish. "It's not a big deal. My mother runs the center, and—"

Diana smiled and said, "Darling, that's wonderful! Don't forget—everyone has to start somewhere. And there are no small parts, only small actors."

I sat up taller. Diana was right.

"That's kind of the way I was thinking of it," I said. "It will be a great way for me to learn more about directing."

Danielle rolled her eyes.

"Exactly," Diana said. "You should get in there and make that play your own. Put your mark on it!"

"I will," I said. "That's exactly what I'm going to do. And my first move will be a casting change."

I glanced across the table at Danielle. "The play depends on a great Wicked Queen. Ashley asked me to play the role—but I'd like you to take over the part if you want to. Will you do it, Danielle?"

Diana beamed. "Do it, Danielle, you'll be wonderful!"

"Okay, I will," Danielle agreed. "It's always fun playing the bad guy. Right, Diana?"

"Right," Diana said.

This is working out great! I thought as Estelle served us coffee and fresh fruit. *Mikki Olsen's* Snow

White and the Seven Dwarfs *is going to be a masterpiece!*

❀

Splash!

"Nice one, Lauren!" I called, clapping.

Lauren had just performed a monster cannon-ball. She climbed out of the pool, tall, pale, and freckle-faced with long, wavy brown hair. But Ben pushed her right back in again. *Splash!*

"These quesadillas are fantastic, Ashley," Brittany said, dipping one in the guacamole. She'd spent all afternoon building sets for the play, and her short, curly brown hair and dark brown skin were still speckled with green paint. "Did you make all this food?"

I nodded. I made all the food before I knew that Mary-Kate wouldn't be here. But why let thirty-five tacos and quesadillas go to waste?

And even without Mary-Kate we managed to have a good time. All our friends were there—Brittany and Lauren, Aaron, Ben, Melanie Han and Tashema Mitchell, and Malcolm Freeman with his new girlfriend, Sophie Curtis.

"Here, Sophie, put these on," Malcolm said. He was trying to slip a pair of duck-shaped swimmies over Sophie's arms. "Really, I'm worried about your safety."

"Malcolm, stop it," Sophie said, laughing. "Whoa!"

She fell backward into the shallow end of the pool, the swimmies on her arms.

"Don't worry, Sophie, I'll save you!" Malcolm cried. He jumped into the pool. He hugged her. "Whew, that was close," he joked. "See, I told you. Good thing you had your swimmies on."

Sophie giggled. "You know, I have my lifesaving certificate, Malcolm," she said. "Maybe *you* should wear the swimmies."

"Me? No." He shook his head. "I've got too much dignity for that. I'd rather drown, thank you."

But he didn't fight Sophie as she slipped the swimmies over his skinny, pale arms.

"How do they look?" he asked her. "Cool?"

"Everything looks cool on you, Malcolm," Sophie said. Malcolm wore them for the rest of the evening.

"Malcolm and Sophie, Ashley's matchmaking masterpiece," Aaron teased. He grinned down at me, tall, dark-haired, blue-eyed, and gorgeous. I still couldn't believe the cutest guy in school was my boyfriend.

"No, *you're* my matchmaking masterpiece," I said. We got together through a dating service I started at Click Café. Ashley's Love Link was now on the Bayside High Website, and it was turning into a huge success.

Aaron kissed me and jumped into the pool.

"It's always fun hanging at your house, Ashley," Brittany said. "Too bad Mary-Kate couldn't be here."

"I'm sure we're having a better time than Mary-Kate is," Lauren said. "What could she do? She couldn't let Danielle down."

Brittany glanced at me and laughed. "Yeah, right. Poor Danielle. I think Mary-Kate's just lost it a little from hanging around movie stars all the time. She'll be back to normal soon, I guess."

"It's really my fault," I said. "I didn't ask Mary-Kate if she was free tonight, and she couldn't get out of her other plans. She says Danielle and her mother get along better when she's around. That's what Danielle tells her, anyway."

Brittany looked skeptical. "If that's true, we might never see Mary-Kate again!"

"Shhh!" Lauren whispered. "Look who's coming!"

Mary-Kate and Danielle breezed over toward the pool wearing matching black satin jackets.

"Hey, Mary-Kate! You made it!" Melanie called.

"Hi, Danielle," I said.

Everyone got out of the pool and ran over to greet them.

"Where did that jacket come from?" I asked Mary-Kate.

"Danielle gave it to me," she said. She turned around to show us the movie logo on the back. Danielle turned, too. The jackets were exactly the same.

"Very cool," Tashema said.

Brittany caught my eye and raised an eyebrow at me. Brittany wasn't crazy about Danielle—and now she and Mary-Kate were wearing matching clothes?

"Are you hungry, Mary-Kate?" I asked. "How about you, Danielle? We've got tons of food left."

"No thanks, we already ate," Mary-Kate said. But then she gave me a look, and I realized I'd forgotten to call her Mikki again.

"Come sit down, Mary-Kate," Lauren said, tugging her toward a lounge chair. "I want to hear all about the movie set."

"First of all, I should tell you that I'm going by a different name now," Mary-Kate announced. "From now on I'd love it if everyone would call me Mikki."

"Isn't it cute?" Danielle added.

Brittany's other eyebrow shot up. I hadn't mentioned Mary-Kate's new name to anyone yet. I was hoping it was gone by now.

"Go get your bathing suit on, Mikki," I said. "The party's still going strong. You can borrow one of our suits if you want, Danielle."

Mary-Kate shook her head. "I'm exhausted," she said.

"I just stopped in to say hello," Danielle added.

"Oh, come on," Lauren protested. "You've been gone for two weeks! So much happened while you were away!"

"Yeah," Brittany agreed. "We need to catch up."

"I've got to go to bed," Mary-Kate insisted.

"And I've got to get home," Danielle added.

"Well, why don't we all go shopping together on Wednesday?" Brittany suggested. "We'll hear about your trip then."

"Sounds good," Mary-Kate agreed. "See you guys later." She walked Danielle to her car. A few minutes later Mary-Kate returned.

Great! I thought. *Now that Danielle is gone, Mary-Kate is going to join us after all!*

"Ashley!" she called. "Can I talk to you a minute?"

I hurried across the lawn to meet her. "What's up?"

"I just wanted to let you know I have so many ideas about the play!" she said. "But before I go any further, we need to talk about casting. What roles have you cast so far?"

"Well, Lauren is playing Snow White, and Ben is the prince," I told her. "The children are playing the dwarfs, the trees, the woodland animals, parts like that. As I said before, I'd like you to be the Wicked Queen and Aaron to play the hunter."

Mary-Kate frowned. "Aaron? Is he a good actor?"

"Well, sure, he's okay," I said. "I needed a guy, and it's not a very big part—"

She knit her brows and thought this over. "I'd like to see Brittany as the hunter," she said. "She's got theater experience. And it will be good for the kids to see a girl in a traditionally male role."

What? "Well, I guess it's not too late to change things, but—"

"Aaron can play a servant or something," Mary-Kate suggested. "Trust me—Brittany will make a great hunter."

I was a little annoyed. The hunter had only a few lines, but Aaron had already memorized them. And I hated to take his part away from him, even though I didn't think he'd mind.

But the longer I thought about it, the more I realized that Mary-Kate's suggestion made sense. As an actor, Aaron was a little stiff, but Brittany was very comfortable onstage.

"We'll have to call a meeting of everybody involved in the play," Mary-Kate went on. "Including Danielle."

"Danielle?" I asked. "What does she have to do with this?"

"She's playing the Wicked Queen," Mary-Kate declared.

"What? No!" I cried. "I want you to be the Wicked Queen."

I remembered when Mary-Kate and Danielle worked on *Grease* together. Mary-Kate came home from rehearsals complaining about what a prima donna Danielle was. Including her in the play seemed like asking for trouble.

"I asked Danielle to do it, and she agreed," Mary-Kate said. "This way, I'll have more time to focus on directing. And who plays wicked better than Danielle Bloom? It's the best thing for everybody."

"You should have talked to me first," I protested.

"I'm sorry," Mary-Kate said. "But I just knew you'd agree once you thought about it. It makes so much sense!"

I had an uneasy feeling as I watched her walk back to the house. Mary-Kate sure was taking this play seriously. I'd wanted her to be involved in it from the beginning. But this was too much. I didn't expect her to take over!

chapter five

"Nice auditorium," Mary-Kate said as she gazed around. "The whole day-care center looks fantastic, Mom."

"Thank you, honey," Mom said, smiling at her. "I have to say, I'm very pleased with it."

Mom had just finished giving Mary-Kate and Danielle a tour of the renovated Sunshine Day Care Center, saving the best for last—the new auditorium. I was already there helping Brittany paint the sets.

"We're in pretty good shape so far," I told Mary-Kate and Danielle. "We've built the sets, and the kids know a lot of their lines already. I think you'll be impressed."

"It's time for rehearsal." Mom checked her watch. "I'll go get the kids now. Wait until you see them—they're adorable!"

Mom left to get the kids. Mary-Kate and Danielle walked up to the stage, where Brittany was putting the finishing touches of paint on the forest set.

The set looked great—tons of thick green trees and a cute little cottage made of painted cardboard for the seven dwarfs, with real furniture and everything. I was very proud of it.

Mary-Kate stared at the stage for several minutes.

"That's the set?" she asked.

Brittany stopped painting and looked up. "Hey, Danielle, Mary-Kate," she said. "What do you think?"

"Hi, Brittany," Danielle said. "Um—she's Mikki now, remember?"

Brittany and I exchanged a glance.

"Oh, right," Brittany said. "How could I forget?"

"Looks like you've been working really hard, Brittany," Mary-Kate said.

Brittany shrugged. "It's fun."

Danielle leaned toward Mary-Kate and started whispering and pointing to different parts of the set.

"Well?" I said. "You haven't said what you think of the set yet."

Mary-Kate sighed. "Well . . . don't you think it's kind of . . . obvious?"

"Obvious?" I asked. "What do you mean?"

Mary-Kate stepped onto the stage. "Look at this forest. It's all green."

"That's the usual color for trees," Brittany said.

"Yes, but what does this forest stand for?" Mary-Kate asked. "What role does it play in the story? What does it represent?"

Brittany stared at Mary-Kate. "It represents a bunch of trees."

"I think I know what Mary-Kate—I mean *Mikki*—is getting at." I was trying to see her point of view even though I didn't agree with it.

I explained, "In the play, the Queen orders the hunter to take Snow White into the forest and kill her. So the forest represents danger."

"Right," Mary-Kate said. "You don't need to paint trees. Everyone knows a forest has trees. Paint the *color*. The *feeling*. Maybe black. Or blood-red."

"*You* paint it blood-red," Brittany snapped. "I just spent two days on this forest, and I'm not doing it over."

"She's just trying to make the play more interesting," Danielle said. "More memorable."

51

"This is a day-care center," Brittany said, "not Broadway."

Mary-Kate turned to her. "That doesn't mean that we have to be obvious or ordinary, does it?"

Brittany rolled her eyes and went back to painting sets.

"Ashley, I really think Mikki is right," Danielle said. "The sets need to be redone. To emphasize the feeling of each scene."

"Redone!" I cried. "We don't have time for that. The play is in a week!"

"Don't worry, Ashley," Mary-Kate said. "We won't completely redo them. We'll just tweak them a little to help bring out the themes of the story."

"Fine," I said. "As long as it's ready in time for the show."

Nobody will be looking at the sets anyway, I told myself. *Everyone will be watching the kids—and the kids will be adorable!*

There was a clatter in the hallway and the kids arrived, led by Mom. They trooped into the auditorium and up to the stage.

"Hey, kids!" I greeted them.

"Hi, Ashley!" they shouted. They sat down on the stage floor.

"They're all yours, Ashley," Mom said. "I'm

taking a coffee break." She waved to the kids and made her way out of the auditorium.

Mary-Kate and Danielle joined me at the front of the stage. "Kids, I want you to meet someone very special," I announced. "This is my sister, Mikki. She's going to help me direct the play. And this is her friend Danielle. She's going to play . . . guess who?"

"The Wicked Queen!" a little boy named Darren called out.

"That's right," I said.

Danielle wrinkled up her face, twisted her hands into claws, and screeched out her witchiest laugh. "A-ha-ha-ha-ha! I'll get you, Snow White!" The kids screamed and giggled. I had to admit, she was pretty good.

"Oooh! She's scary! She's like a witch!" Darren shouted.

"Mikki and Danielle know a lot about putting on plays," I told the kids. "Let's show them the scene we practiced the other day. Remember? I need my seven dwarfs. Stand up, dwarfs."

The dwarfs stood up. "All right, Mary-Ka— Mikki," I said, pointing to each child in turn. "Meet the dwarfs!"

Mary-Kate grinned. "I can't wait to see your work," she said to them.

Their work? They were preschoolers!

"Okay, kids," I said, leading the dwarfs backstage and lining them up. "Remember, this is the beginning of the story. The dwarfs are marching home from the mines. They are going home to their cottage in the forest. They are unhappy because the cottage is all messy and none of the dwarfs knows how to cook or clean. Okay, begin."

Mary-Kate, Danielle, Brittany, and I watched as the kids rehearsed their scene. They all looked so serious—and cute!—as they said their lines. A few of them had to be reminded what their lines were, but that was understandable. I caught Danielle and Mary-Kate whispering a few times.

When the scene was over, I grinned at Brittany. She gave me a thumbs-up.

"All right, all right," I said, clapping my hands to get their attention. "We'll stop there for now. When Lauren gets here, we can rehearse some more." I turned to Mary-Kate. "What do you think?"

"Cute," Mary-Kate said. "But I think we can handle the scene a little differently and get a lot more out of it."

"What do you mean?" I asked.

"Let me talk to them," Mary-Kate offered. "I can help them with their line readings. I learned a lot from watching the kids on the set of Diana's movie. They all had acting coaches."

"Well, we can't afford acting coaches," I said.

"That's okay," Mary-Kate said. "I'll do it for free."

"I'm thirsty," Danielle said. "Is there a soda machine around here?"

"Down the hall in the teachers' lounge," I told her, pointing the way.

"Be right back," she said.

Mary-Kate clapped her hands. "Great job, kids!" she said. "Everybody, gather over here. I want to talk to you for a minute."

The kids gathered around Mary-Kate.

"You are all such good little actors!" Mary-Kate said. "But I'm going to teach you some things that will help you be even better."

"This should be good," Brittany whispered to me. She snickered.

"You have to use the Method," Mary-Kate told the kids. "Do you all know what the Method is?"

Blank stares from the kids. How could they possibly know what she was talking about? I didn't.

"The Method is when you don't just *pretend* to be a dwarf or a tree or a bunny rabbit," Mary-Kate explained. "You *are* a dwarf. Or a tree or whatever.

You think about your character. Then you reach deep down inside you and find the character there."

She pointed to a boy named Silas. "You play the sleepy dwarf, right?" she asked him.

"Right," Silas said.

"So somewhere inside you, you have a sleepy, sleepy dwarf just waiting to come out. Close your eyes and see him in your mind. When you find him, bring him up to the surface. It's just like he's underwater, and he pops up for air."

Silas looked scared. "There's a dwarf inside me? Get him out! Get him out!"

"It's nothing to be scared of," Mary-Kate said, patting Silas. "We all have them inside of us. We have all kinds of people inside us. We just have to find them."

A little girl said, "My dwarf just burped."

"Good," Mary-Kate said. "Now we're getting somewhere."

"I don't believe this," Brittany whispered to me.

It was pretty ridiculous—and I wasn't so sure it was working. I interrupted Mary-Kate.

"Mikki, where did you get all this?" I asked. "About the Method, I mean."

"From the book Tyler gave me," she replied, "and from some of the exercises Steven did with the

56

actors on the set. It's a classic acting technique."

"I'm not sure the kids are getting it," I said. "Why don't you try working with them one-on-one? Pick whichever child you think you can help the most."

"All right." Mary-Kate scanned the group of children. "The grouchy dwarf needs work. She's way too happy. Let me talk to her. I'll deal with the shy dwarf later."

Deal with?

"Okay, Mikki," I said, "but remember—they're only little kids." I called to the girl who played the grouchy dwarf. "Come here a minute, please, Hannah. Mikki wants to talk to you."

Hannah marched over and sat on the stage beside Mary-Kate. "Hi, Hannah," Mary-Kate said. "How are you?"

"Fine," Hannah said.

"No, Hannah, you're not fine," Mary-Kate told her.

"I am too fine," Hannah insisted. "And I'm special, too."

"Yes, yes, you're special," Mary-Kate said. "But you're also grouchy, remember? You're the grouchy dwarf. Everything stinks! You're always in a bad mood!"

"I'm not grouchy," Hannah protested. "I'm happy!"

"But you are *playing* the grouchy dwarf," Mary-Kate said. "You've got to really get into your part. You have to *be* grouchy deep down inside. Think for a minute. What is your motivation?"

Hannah looked confused. "I don't know that word," she said.

I nudged Mary-Kate. "Um—Mikki—don't you think you're being a little—"

Mary-Kate ignored me and pressed on.

"Close your eyes and think," she told Hannah. "Why is the grouchy dwarf so grouchy? What made her that way? Maybe something happened to her a long time ago. Something she can never forget—"

Hannah stared up at Mary-Kate. "I forgot to wash my hands before I ate my lunch."

Mary-Kate sighed. "Let's try this. What makes *you* feel grouchy, Hannah?"

Hannah thought for a minute. "When my sister eats all the cookies," she said.

"Good, good," Mary-Kate said. "So when you get up on that stage, keep thinking about that. Think, 'My sister ate all the cookies! That's why I'm so grouchy!' Okay?"

"Okay," Hannah said. Then she toddled back to

the other dwarfs. "My sister ate all the cookies! That's why I'm grouchy!" she announced.

"Are you sure this is such a good idea?" I asked Mary-Kate. "I mean, Hannah's only four. I think you're confusing her."

"Listen, Ashley, I know what I'm doing. You'll see," Mary-Kate said. "I'll work with each of the kids individually—even the animals. By the time you put on this play, it will have more depth and texture than you ever dreamed!"

"Depth?" I echoed. "Texture? This is a play at a day-care center!"

"Let's try the scene again," Mary-Kate said to the kids. They lined up. Hannah still wore her usual happy grin. "Remember, Hannah—your sister ate all the cookies!"

Hannah immediately frowned. For the first time onstage, she finally did look grouchy.

Hmmm . . . I thought. *Maybe Mikki's Method is working after all. It* would *be nice to have the grouchy dwarf look grouchy once in a while.*

Danielle returned with her soda. She stood at the back of the room, studying the set. "We have *got* to do something about that background, Mikki," she called. "And the lighting!"

Mary-Kate stared at the stage lights overhead.

"You're right," she said, turning to me. "I'll take care of that, Ashley. I'm sure I can come up with something."

"Oh, good," Brittany joked. "What's a preschool play without professional sets and lighting? You might as well not even put it on!"

I giggled. Mary-Kate cast a sidelong glance at us. "I'm just trying to help," she said.

Lauren arrived for rehearsal.

"Hey, am I late?" she said.

"No, we're just about to run through the cottage scene again," I told her. "We'll start where you come in."

Lauren jumped up onstage.

"All right, kids," I called. "Get ready. Here comes Snow White!"

The kids giggled. They loved Lauren.

"Don't forget, kids!" Mary-Kate added. "The Method! Motivation!"

They played the scene where the dwarfs come home from work to find their cottage all cleaned up. Then they find Snow White asleep in one of their beds. She wakes up and meets them for the first time.

Mary-Kate and Danielle stood in the back, whispering the whole time. Mary-Kate jotted down notes.

Suddenly, right in the middle of one of Lauren's lines, Mary-Kate called out, "Hold it! Hold it!" She ran up to the stage. Everyone stopped.

"Lauren, don't forget that Snow White is sort of a motherly figure to the dwarfs," Mary-Kate said. "So when the sneezy dwarf sneezes and you say 'Gesundheit,' it should be a little more serious. More like a mother would say it than like a friend."

"What?" Lauren looked at me as if to say, *Is she serious?* Brittany stepped backstage so Mary-Kate wouldn't see her cracking up.

I shrugged.

"Like this?" Lauren asked. She lowered her voice so it sounded deeper. "Gesundheit."

"Better, better," Mary-Kate said.

"Even deeper if you can," Danielle added.

Oh, brother! I thought. Or should I say *Oh, sister!* Mikki was driving me crazy! We'd never get through rehearsal at this rate.

Keep calm, I told myself as I watched Mary-Kate scribble down more notes. *Mom is counting on you to do a good job with this play. And some of Mikki's ideas are good. So just hang on until it's over—if you can.*

chapter six

"**W**ell, darlings, what did you think of that interview?" Diana asked.

Diana, Danielle, and I were coming back to their house after meeting with a journalist in a hotel suite. Diana said she didn't want to let the reporter in her house—he might snoop around too much.

"You were great," I told her. "I liked the way you made jokes when the reporter asked about your personal life. You really had him under control."

"Thank you, darling." Diana smiled at me. "That's a specialty of mine."

Diana disappeared into the study, and Danielle and I headed up to her room.

"Can I use your computer for a few minutes?" I asked Danielle. "I'm researching different productions of *Snow White*, looking for inspiration."

"Go ahead," Danielle said. She flopped onto her bed and opened up a magazine. "The Sunshine Day Care version needs all the help it can get."

"Thanks." I logged on to the Internet using my new screen name, Stella, after a character in the famous American play *A Streetcar Named Desire*.

"Knock, knock," Diana said from the doorway. "I'm not interrupting any secret girl talk, am I, darlings?"

"No, Diana," Danielle said. "Come on in."

"I just wanted to remind you that I'm going shopping tomorrow, Danielle," Diana said. "For the publicity tour. So if you need anything—"

Danielle yawned. "Where are you going?"

"I thought I'd start at Carucci," Diana said.

"Carucci! Wow," I said. "I've always wanted to shop there."

Carucci was one of the chicest stores in Beverly Hills. Mom said it was too expensive.

"Well then, why don't you come with, darling?" Diana said. "We'd love to have you along."

Shopping with Diana Donovan—cool! But then I remembered something—I promised Brittany I'd go shopping with her and Ashley and Lauren that day.

"I thought it would be just the two of us," Danielle said to Diana.

"You know, I just remembered," I said. "I can't go. I promised my sister and our friends I'd go shopping with them tomorrow."

"Oh, darling, just tell them you're busy," Diana said. "I'm sure they won't mind."

"Well, I guess so . . ." I said.

"Lovely. We'll pick you up at noon tomorrow," Diana said. She breezed out.

"I need a soda," Danielle said. She got up and stomped out of the room.

I sat staring at the computer screen for a minute. Shopping at Carucci with Diana Donovan! It was like something out of a magazine!

Ding! Someone IM'd me. Tyler!

TYNYC44: Mikster, is that you? What's up, girl?

I panicked. What's up? What would the fabulous Mikki be up to? Researching *Snow White* for a kiddie play?

I don't think so.

STELLA1616: Hey Tyler. Just hanging with Danielle. We went to the Four Seasons with Diana for an interview with Vamp *Magazine. What are you doing?*

TYNYC44: Watching Daisy and Emma. And reading this great interview with Lars Hansen in Film Arts Magazine. *The guy is such a genius. He maps out the first scene in* Interplay *shot by shot.*
STELLA1616: Cool.

What else could I say? I still hadn't seen *Interplay*.

TYNYC44: What have you been up to since you got back to Cali? Seen any good movies lately?

No, I hadn't. I hadn't done much besides hang out with Diana and Danielle and work on the play at the Sunshine Day Care Center. But that would sound so lightweight to a serious film guy like Tyler. Think, Mikki, think!

TYNYC44: Mikki, you still there???

Maybe I *could* tell him about the play—just leave out certain little details. Like the fact that it stars a bunch of four-year-olds.

STELLA1616: I'm directing a play! It's very exciting. Working with a lot of new young actors. It's based on Snow White *but I'm trying to bring out the—*

I paused, thinking. The what? What was I trying to bring out?

—the subtext. You know, the deeper meaning behind the story.
TYNYC44: Excellent. Fairy tales are full of subtext. When's the play? What theater?
STELLA1616: Next week. It's in a small community theater.
TYNYC44: Too cool. Good luck with it, Mikster. Check you later.
STELLA1616: Over and out.

I logged off, relieved. Whew! Being Mikki takes some quick thinking, I realized. But it's worth it. Now Tyler thinks I'm a serious theater intellectual and not just a glorified baby-sitter.

And that was exactly what I wanted him to think. The truth was just too embarrassing.

chapter seven

"Miss Donovan, hello. Welcome to Carucci of Beverly Hills. My name is Tiffani."

A sleek, well-dressed saleswoman greeted Diana, Danielle, and me as soon as we walked into the shop. She led us to a plush sitting area with magazines, chocolate, and fresh fruit on the table. "Can I get you something to drink? A glass of chardonnay, perhaps?"

"Just some iced green tea with a splash of peach nectar, thank you," Diana ordered. "Lemon on the side. Girls?" She turned to Danielle and me.

I nodded at Danielle. "We'll have the same," she said.

I tried to act as if I shopped in fabulous designer boutiques like this all the time, but it was hard not to stare. The front of the store was spare and modern and comfortable, but the dressing rooms in the back were like fancy hotel rooms. The saleswomen were perfectly made up and sharply dressed in Carucci clothes. Most of the shoppers looked like movie stars or rich Beverly Hills wives.

This beats the mall any day, I thought, and then felt a pang of guilt. I was supposed to be at the mall with Ashley, Brittany, and Lauren that very moment. But I told my friends I was going to the studio for more post-production work and would go to the mall another day. I felt bad about lying to them. But going to the mall was no big deal. Shopping with a movie star didn't happen every day. Not to me, at least.

Diana took off her coat, and Tiffani immediately took it from her and hung it up in a dressing room. "Oooh, look at these," Diana said as she made a beeline for a rack of sheer silk print dresses. She held one up against her body and posed in front of the mirror.

Danielle sat down on a couch and picked out a chocolate. A sales assistant brought our drinks and set them on the table.

I ignored my drink and looked through a rack of tops. They were so beautiful. Then—"Ow!" My fingernail caught on a hanger.

"What happened?" Tiffani asked.

"No big deal," I said. "I just chipped a nail."

Tiffani took my hand and studied the broken nail. "Let me call a manicurist for you," she offered. "We can have that nail fixed in no time."

She wanted to call a manicurist? Just to fix my broken nail? I glanced at Danielle, who didn't seem surprised by this offer at all.

"Go ahead," Danielle said. "I've done it before."

"That's all right," I said. "I can fix it at home."

"Just let me know if you change your mind," Tiffani said. She took a green dress from Diana. "Let me put that in your dressing room for you."

"I think that dress is too young for you," Danielle said to Diana.

"Don't be silly, Danielle," Diana said. "I'm only thirty-five. That might seem old to you at sixteen, but trust me, it's not."

Danielle rolled her eyes, and I had the feeling Diana was probably older than she said. But she was in great shape and looked good in everything.

"Let's see," Diana said, heading for another rack. "I definitely need some pants." She picked out four pairs of skinny pants in different colors.

I found myself drawn to a rack of silk dresses, all in different shades of blue. I looked through them carefully, admiring each one. I sighed.

"Diana, I'm hungry," Danielle complained.

"We'll stop for lunch after we leave here," Diana said. But Tiffani was immediately at Danielle's side with a menu of spa foods.

"I'll take a smoothie," Danielle ordered. "But I really want a Vietnamese summer roll."

"We can get that for you if you like," Tiffani said.

"You know what? Cancel the whole order," Danielle said. "I'll just wait."

I couldn't believe the way Tiffani was ready to get us anything we wanted, whether they had it in the store or not. I thought of the surly salesgirls at the mall. Their attitude was more like "If you're not going to buy something, get out."

I could get used to this, I thought.

Danielle finally got up off the couch and started pawing through a rack of skirts. Diana disappeared into the dressing room to try things on.

I pulled a blue silk Indian-print halter dress off the rack. It sparkled with sequins. It was a very special dress—perfect for a big event, like a movie opening.

"Would you like to try that on?" Tiffani asked me. "It's just your style."

Why not? It wouldn't hurt to see how it looked.

"All right," I agreed. Tiffani led me to a dressing room.

I tried on the dress and stared at myself in the mirror. It was gorgeous! And it made me look so glamorous! I could hardly take my eyes off myself.

"How are you doing in there?" Tiffani asked. I opened the dressing room door. She smiled and said, "That looks lovely on you. Come out and show your friend."

I stepped out of the dressing room to model for Danielle. She stood at a counter, poking through handbags. Diana was trying on a jacket nearby.

"What do you think?" I asked.

Diana looked up. "Darling, it's perfect for you!" she declared. "You have to get it."

Danielle crossed her arms, studied me, and sighed. "You're crazy if you don't buy that dress," she pronounced.

I checked myself out in the mirror again. I had to admit, the dress was fantastic. It fit me perfectly, brought out the blue in my eyes, and was completely chic.

"Diana, I need a new bag," Danielle said. She dumped a $1,500 leather bag on the counter. "And these T-shirts. And this skirt."

She dropped the clothes on top of the bag. The hangers clattered.

"All right, darling," Diana said, but she wasn't really paying attention. She was too busy checking out the leather jackets.

"You've got to get this dress," Tiffani said to me. "It looks fantastic on you."

"Maybe I will," I said. I reached around to find the price tag. But when I looked at the price, I thought I was going to faint!

How could one dress cost so much? I'd have to clean out my savings account to pay for it—all my Christmas and birthday money, plus six months' allowance!

Danielle appeared beside me with five pairs of sunglasses stacked on her head. I was standing in front of the mirror, staring at the dress, paralyzed with indecision. I wanted it so badly . . . but it cost so much! . . . but it was so perfect for me . . . but it cost so much! . . .

"Are you going to get that dress or not?" Danielle asked.

"Get it, darling," Diana said. "I mean, why not?" She pulled two leather jackets off their hangers and added, "I'd better get this in black *and* brown."

Because it costs way, way too much money, I

thought. But I was too embarrassed to admit that to Diana and Danielle. They were buying whatever they wanted! And they never thought about how much things cost.

Tiffani brought over a bag, a pair of high-heeled sandals, and a silver pendant. "Try these with the dress," she urged me. "Then you'll really see how fabulous it can look."

She draped the pendant over my neck, hung the small leather bag over my shoulder, and dropped the sandals on the floor in front of me.

I slipped my feet into the shoes. She was right. Now the dress looked even more glamorous than before. It was as if I were transformed into a completely different person—a much more fabulous person than the everyday Mary-Kate. I was Mikki!

"I'm getting these jackets, plus the pants and the dress in my dressing room," Diana told Tiffani, dumping the jackets into her arms. She looked me over and added, "Mikki darling, you look adorable! If you buy that dress, I'll give you those accessories to go with it. My treat."

I gasped. She was going to buy me a bag, a pendant, and a pair of Carucci shoes?

"You're going to buy all that stuff for her?" Danielle asked.

"Diana, I can't let you do that," I protested.

"Why not? It's only money," Diana said.

What could I say? It was all too much for me. I couldn't resist any longer.

"All right," I said. "I'll get the dress."

Tiffani beamed. "You won't regret it."

"And I'm getting all this stuff," Danielle said, pointing to the towering pile of clothes on the counter and the five pairs of sunglasses on her head.

I gave my credit card to Tiffani. "I'll go ring this up," she said. She called another saleswoman to take away the rest of clothes.

I went back to the dressing room and changed into my regular clothes—a yellow cotton sundress which suddenly felt totally blah.

I guess I won't be getting an iPod this year, I thought as I imagined what my credit-card bill would look like. *But that's okay. This dress is totally Mikki.*

I had no idea how expensive it was to be fabulous! But it was worth it—right?

Easy, easy, I said to myself as I tiptoed down the hallway toward my room. Danielle had dropped me off at home just before dinner. Ashley was sure to be back from the mall by now. I wanted to make it into my room before she saw me with my Carucci shopping bags.

I crept past Ashley's room. Almost there . . .

"Hey!" Ashley popped her head out of her room. "You're back! How was the post-production thing?"

I froze. Ashley's eyes fell on the shopping bags.

"Where did you get those? Carucci?" she asked.

She must have noticed the guilty look in my eyes. She frowned and crossed her arms.

"I . . . um . . ." I stammered.

"You went shopping?" she cried. "What happened to the studio? Learning all about film editing?"

"Well, I—" I tried to think of something to say. I knew I could say we went shopping after we left the studio. But Ashley was giving me her laser X-ray glare. I couldn't lie to her—she'd see right through it. And I didn't want to lie, anyway.

"Diana wanted to go shopping," I explained. "And she said I could go, too—"

"I can't believe this," Ashley interrupted. "You promised me and Lauren and Brittany you'd go shopping with us today to make up for not hanging with us the other night, remember? And then you blow us off to go shopping with Diana Donovan?"

"Ashley, you don't understand," I said. "How often do I get the chance to go shopping with a superstar? If you wanted to do something special like that, I wouldn't want to hold you back just for a trip to the mall."

Ashley frowned. "I guess so," she said. "Let me see what you bought."

She followed me into my room and I opened up the bags. "Diana gave me these as a gift," I said as I pulled out the bag, the pendant, and the shoes.

"Wow!" Ashley gasped, admiring the accessories. "Some gift!"

"She bought them to go with this," I said, bringing out the dress with a flourish.

"It's totally gorgeous," Ashley said, staring at the dress. "But it's so fancy! When would you ever wear it?"

"I could wear it on a date," I said, trying to convince myself.

"Sure—on a date with Prince William," Ashley joked. She reached for the price tag. I tried to jerk the dress away before she saw it. Too late.

She stared at the tag, her mouth hanging open, for a full minute.

"Mary-Kate, are you nuts?" she finally shrieked. "This is more than six months' allowance! You spent all that money on one dress? One dress that you'll never have a chance to wear in your whole life?"

"Ashley, you don't understand," I repeated.

More and more I felt like that was true—my life was changing and Ashley didn't understand it. "I *need* this dress. The way things are going I probably *will* have a chance to wear it somewhere. And I might need more like it!"

"For what?" Ashley asked. "The first day of school?"

"You're jealous!" I snapped. "You're jealous because I'm out with Diana having all these wonderful experiences, while you're—" I stopped.

"What?" Ashley demanded. "While I'm what? Sitting at home like a jerk twiddling my thumbs? Is that what you're saying?"

"No! Of course not," I said. "It's just . . . well, I *have* been meeting a lot of interesting people lately, and—"

"I'm not jealous of you," Ashley insisted. "Not at all. I just don't like what's happening to you— *Mikki*."

She stalked back to her room and shut the door. *She* is *jealous*, I thought. *What's happening to me is I'm becoming a lot more sophisticated.*

I slipped off my sundress and tried on the Carucci dress again. It looked even better than before.

This dress is so Mikki, I thought as I admired the dress in the mirror. *If Ashley can't understand that, that's her problem.*

chapter eight

The kids will cheer me up, I thought as I walked into the day-care center the next afternoon. *They always do.*

I headed to the auditorium for another rehearsal of *Snow White*, grumbling to myself. Things were still tense between Mary-Kate and me. She hardly spoke to me all morning.

And it's all because of a dress, I thought sadly. *That's so silly! We've got to straighten this out.*

Then I walked into the auditorium and saw the set. "What happened in here?" I gasped.

All the trees in the forest had been painted black. And the black leaves had red spots dripping down from them—like they were crying bloody tears! It was the most depressing set I'd ever seen.

Then I remembered—Mary-Kate said she and

Danielle were going to "tweak" the set. What was Mary-Kate thinking? Bloody trees?

"My set!" a voice cried from the back of the room. "What have they done to my beautiful forest!"

I turned around. Brittany and Lauren had just come in. Brittany ran up to the stage and stared at it in horror.

"Ashley, what happened?" Lauren asked. "Did someone spill paint on the set?"

"It's Mikki," I explained. "She and Danielle repainted it."

"It's hideous," Brittany said. "What is she trying to do?"

I shook my head. "I have no idea."

"Hey, guys, what do you think?" Mary-Kate burst into the auditorium. "Amazing, huh? Now the forest really *looks* like something, you know? Like the dark night of the soul . . ."

We turned and watched her stride toward the stage. She was wearing all black—black pants, black turtleneck—with a long red silk scarf fluttering behind her as she walked. Her smile faded when she saw the looks on our faces.

"What's wrong?" she asked. "Is it the trees? They're not dark enough, are they? I meant to give them two coats of black paint, but we ran out—"

"That's not the problem," Brittany snapped. "The problem is the trees look weird. Very, very weird."

"Weird is *good*," Mary-Kate insisted. "It goes with the story. Think about it—this queen talks to a mirror every day to make sure she's the fairest one of all. And the mirror talks back! The queen is so jealous of her pretty stepdaughter that she tries to have her killed! So the girl runs away into the forest and meets seven dwarfs who take her in. Her stepmother finds her and gives her a poisoned apple, and the girl goes to sleep. But then a prince comes along and kisses her and she wakes up. I mean, if that's not weird, what is?"

"That's one way to look at it, I guess," I said. "But on the other hand, it's just *Snow White*. A fairy tale everybody knows. Starring a bunch of cute little kids. You don't have to think so hard about it."

"Last time I checked, Snow White lived in a world with green trees," Brittany added, "that didn't cry tears of blood, or any kind of tears at all."

Mary-Kate pressed her lips together. "Danielle and I worked hard on this set," she said. "We were just trying to add another layer to the play. To give it some texture."

"Well, I worked hard on the set, too," Brittany

shot back. "And I was trying to make it look nice for the kids and their parents. I don't think anyone's coming to the Sunshine Day-care Center looking for a layered, textured experience at the theater. They just want to see their kids in a play! That's *all*!"

"I'm trying to give them something better than that!" Mary-Kate argued. "Maybe you just don't understand."

"Oh, I understand," Brittany said. "I understand that when those kids' parents come in here and see that set, they're going to freak out."

The auditorium door opened and the kids trooped in behind Mom.

"Here they come," Mary-Kate said. "We'll see who freaks out."

"Eeww!" Darren shouted, pointing at the stage. "What happened to the trees?"

"Somebody made them all ugly!" a girl cried.

"Why are they black?" another girl asked. "What's that red stuff coming off them?"

"It looks like puke!" said a boy.

"What happened here, girls?" Mom asked. "Where's Brittany's beautiful set?"

Mary-Kate's face turned red. I felt bad for her. I could tell she was embarrassed. She glanced at Brittany as if she expected her to toss out a smart remark. But Brittany was too nice to say anything.

I thought Mary-Kate might apologize or something. But instead she clapped her hands and said, "Okay, everybody, let's start the rehearsal!"

Mom glanced at me. "Everything under control here, Ashley?" she asked.

"It's fine, Mom," I said. "Go ahead and take a lunch break. We'll be okay."

Mom left. Mary-Kate lined the kids up, ready for the first dwarf scene. "Remember, Hannah," she said to the grouchy dwarf. "Your sister ate all the cookies. There are none left for you. You're very grumpy."

"I've been practicing that," Hannah said, frowning. "I think about my sister and the cookies all the time!"

"Good," Mary-Kate said. "Okay, begin."

The children played out the scene. Brittany, as the hunter, comes to the dwarfs' cottage looking for Snow White. The dwarfs hide Snow White and tell the hunter they don't know where she is.

Brittany went up to the door of the cottage and knocked. "Who's there?" the sneezy dwarf asked. "Ah-choo!"

"The Queen's hunter," Brittany replied.

The sneezy dwarf tried to open the cottage door,

but it stuck. Hannah, as the grouchy dwarf, suddenly shouted, "I want some cookies, and I want them now!" She shoved the sneezy dwarf out of the way and yanked open the door.

"Ow!" cried the sneezy dwarf. "She pushed me! Ah-choo!"

"Give me cookies!" Hannah yelled at Brittany.

"Cut!" called Mary-Kate. "I mean, stop!"

But Hannah didn't stop. She charged into Brittany. "I'm grouchy! I want cookies!"

"Calm down, Hannah." Brittany caught the little girl. Mary-Kate ran up onstage.

"Hannah, you're being grouchy, and that's good," Mary-Kate said. "But you have to stay in the play."

"Not without cookies!" Hannah squealed.

I dropped my head in my hands. Mary-Kate had created a Method-acting monster in Hannah. She had always been so sweet and happy. Now she was angry and obsessed with cookies.

"Could someone please go get some cookies?" Mary-Kate called out.

"I'm on it," Lauren volunteered. "Be right back."

"Look, Lauren is going to get some cookies," Mary-Kate said. "Let's practice the scene again until she comes back."

Hannah scowled at her. Brittany sighed and shook her head.

I ran up onstage. "Hannah, come here a second," I said, beckoning to her. She toddled over to me. I gave her a hug, and she calmed down a little.

"You're such a good dwarf," I told her. "Don't think about cookies so much. Just remember what you're supposed to say."

She calmed down a little. "What am I supposed to say? Something about cookies?"

"No. You're supposed to say, 'Snow White? Never heard of her.' Okay?"

Hannah nodded and repeated the line. She even smiled a little.

"Okay," Mary-Kate called. "Let's try it again."

They played the scene again. Hannah was much better this time. Brittany was speaking her lines, "The Queen has sent me to find Snow White. Have you seen her?" when Mary-Kate interrupted.

"Hold it, hold it," Mary-Kate said. "Brittany, could you try that line a different way? Like this, 'Have *you* seen her?' "

"That sounds stupid," Brittany complained. "It should be 'Have you *seen* her?' "

"Just try it my way and see how it sounds," Mary-Kate insisted. " 'Have *you* seen her?' "

85

"Have *you* seen her?" Brittany said.

"I think that's better," Mary-Kate said.

"No, it isn't better," Brittany snapped. "It sounds ridiculous. It's totally wrong."

"If you could sit out here and listen to it, I think you'd understand," Mary-Kate said.

"Listen, *Mikki*," Brittany said. "Ever since you got home from that movie, you've been a total pain in the neck. First you ruin my set, then you make the kids act weird, and then you criticize the way I say the simplest line. I can't take it anymore. I quit!"

She stomped off the stage and headed out of the auditorium.

"Brittany, no!" I cried. I started to run after her.

"I need a break," Mary-Kate grumbled. She stormed out too. Hannah burst into tears, then Darren started crying, and Lauren wasn't back with the cookies yet. I had to take care of Hannah and Darren before the whole group of dwarfs started wailing their little heads off.

"Why is everybody fighting?" Hannah sobbed. "When do I get a cookie?"

I hugged the children and dried their tears. "Everything's okay," I told them.

But that was a lie. The play was in worse shape

now than it was a few days earlier. At this rate, we'd never be ready in time!

And it was all because of Mary-Kate. I had to find a way to stop her before she totally ruined the play!

What a disaster, I thought as I slumped at my desk. I never realized that working with little kids— and my friends and Ashley—would be so hard.

I logged on to the Internet and started surfing, looking for new ideas for *Snow White*. No one except Danielle seemed to like the ideas I'd had so far. Rehearsal that afternoon had been a total waste. And I couldn't believe Brittany walked out on the play—just because I asked her to say one line a little differently! Talk about a prima donna! It was very unprofessional of her.

My friends don't understand me, I thought. *But Tyler does. . . .*

Maybe I'll IM him and see what he thinks, I decided.

STELLA1616: Hi, Tyler, what are you up to?
TYNYC44: Not much, Mikster, what's happening? I was just about to E-mail you. How's the play going?

STELLA1616: I'm having trouble. The cast doesn't understand what I'm trying to do. One of my actresses actually quit today because I suggested a different line reading to her!

TYNYC44: That stinks. Actresses can be a real pain.

STELLA1616: Tell me about it. I'm so frustrated and I don't know what to do!

TYNYC44: Stay strong, Mikki. Stick to your vision. You're smart and I know your ideas are good.

STELLA1616: Thanks.

TYNYC44: Good news. Dad's coming to Los Angeles this weekend to do some press for Killer Boyfriend—*and I'm coming with him. We should get together.*

STELLA1616: Excellent! When will you get here?

TYNYC44: Saturday afternoon. We'll be in town till Wednesday, so I'll be able to see your play Monday night!

Oh, no! I thought. *He wants to see the play!*

I couldn't let him do that. He thought I was working with some kind of experimental theater group, not four year olds at a day-care center! He'd think I was a total loser!

I had to stop him from coming to the play.

TYNYC44: Hey, Mikki. You still there?

STELLA1616: Still here. I was just checking to see if there are any tickets left for Snow White. *Looks like we're sold out. Sorry.*

TYNYC44: Come on, you're the director! You can't get me a couple of tickets? I'll stand in the back—or even watch from backstage if you want.

Backstage! That was even worse!

STELLA1616: I don't want you to stand through the whole show. You really don't have to come to the show just for me. Why don't we get together afterward? Or on another day? I'm sure you've got better things to do. . . .

TYNYC44: Are you crazy? I can't wait to see your play. I wouldn't miss it. Don't worry, I'll be there, and Dad, too, if he has time.

Now Kyle McGuire was coming too? This was getting worse by the minute!

chapter nine

"**I** hope you girls won't be bored," Diana said. "These photo shoots can drag on forever."

I was sitting beside her in the front seat of her white Mercedes convertible. Danielle was in the backseat. Diana picked us up from the studio, where we'd spent the morning watching the film editor cut and edit *Killer Boyfriend*. Now Diana was going to be photographed for a fashion magazine and Danielle and I were tagging along. Danielle didn't want to go at first, but Diana talked her into it.

"The editor showed us one of the scary scenes," I told Diana. "He used all these quick camera cuts to build tension. It was really terrifying."

"Yeah," Danielle added. "There's a close-up of your face that's going to give me nightmares for weeks, Diana."

Diana cast a sharp, impatient glance back at Danielle. I just kept still and hoped they wouldn't try to drag me into a fight.

"Are you all ready for the movie opening tonight, darling?" Diana asked Danielle. They were going to the opening of a new movie called *Sweet Marie*. "What are you going to wear?"

"I don't know," Danielle said. "I'll figure it out when we get home."

"I wish I could go," I said. "It sounds so exciting! Walking down the red carpet and everything . . ."

"Come with us, Mikki," Diana offered. "You can wear your new dress."

"Really? That would be fantastic!" I cried. I couldn't believe it! I was going to a movie opening with Diana Donovan!

"Be at our house at six-thirty," Diana said. "The limo will take us from there."

"Great," I said. A chance to wear my new dress already!

"How's *Snow White* going, darlings?" Diana asked. "Are you going to be ready in time?"

"Not exactly," I admitted. "But I've been working hard on it. Everyone knows the story of Snow White, so I want to find a new way of telling it."

"Sounds *thrilling*," Diana said. "It's wonderful to

see you so very enthusiastic about the theater."

"We still have a lot of work to do," I said. *That's putting it mildly,* I thought. Ashley managed to talk Brittany into coming back to the play, but the kids were still having trouble remembering their lines. And we were still fighting about the sets.

"Can we talk about something else?" Danielle whined from the backseat.

"Danielle's really great as the Wicked Queen," I told Diana.

"Did you ever think of telling some of the story through dance?" Diana suggested. "Danielle is a wonderful dancer."

"I didn't know that," I said. "But it's a good idea." I made a note on my script, which I kept in my bag. "What do you think about that, Danielle?" I asked.

"I'm dying for a latte," Danielle said. "Can we stop at Click?"

Click! That was the last place I wanted to go. Lauren had just called me on my cell phone to see if I wanted to meet everybody there this afternoon. I told her I was busy working on the play. If she and Ashley and everyone else saw me in the car with Diana and Danielle—well, they might get the wrong idea. And Danielle knew it.

"Why don't we stop at Quick Cup?" I suggested. "It's right up here on the corner. Click's not really on our way."

"Mikki's right, darling," Diana said. "Or you can get coffee at the photo shoot."

"No," Danielle insisted. "Click has the best lattes. We have to go there."

I turned around to look at her. "Why are you doing this?" I asked.

She shrugged. "I just want a good latte. That's all." Her voice was getting shrill.

"All right, Danielle, we'll stop at Click," Diana said. "Let's not go crazy here."

She made a right and drove toward Click. The closer we got, the more nervous I felt. *Maybe Ashley and those guys won't be there yet,* I hoped. *Or maybe they're sitting in the back and won't see me.*

But it was a beautiful, sunny afternoon, and deep down I knew my friends would be there, and I knew where they'd be sitting—at an outside table. With a good view of the parking lot. And me.

❀

"What do you think about Malcolm and Sophie, Ashley?" Brittany asked me.

We were sitting at an outdoor table at Click, waiting for Lauren to join us. Malcolm was inside, working behind the coffee bar. Sophie was his new girlfriend—and I fixed them up myself, thank you very much.

"I think it's great," I said. "Did you hear Malcolm in there? He was actually whistling."

Brittany giggled. "I know. But did you catch what song he was whistling? 'Froggy Went a Courtin'.'"

"That's his favorite song," I explained.

She shook her head. "He's nuts. Anyway, I like Sophie. She's nice."

"Hey, guys," Lauren said as she walked up to our table. "Sorry I'm late. I called Mary-Kate a little while ago to see if she wanted to meet us."

"And—?" I asked.

"She's busy," Lauren reported. "Play stuff."

Brittany shook her head. "I wonder what she's going to do to the play now. Translate it into Japanese?"

"It's weird," I said, sipping my iced coffee. "Almost as if changing your name can change your personality."

"I know," Brittany agreed. "I love Mary-Kate. But I'm not so crazy about Mikki. She acts like her ideas are the only ones that count!"

"I'll admit she's gone too far," I said, "but what can we do? I know she means well."

"I think we should say something to her," Brittany suggested. "Before she really gets out of control."

"I think we're being a little too hard on her," Lauren said. "After all, what has she really done? She's worked very hard to make the play as good as it can be. We might not agree with her ideas, but all she's doing is trying to help us."

"Well, I don't know what she's *trying* to do," Brittany complained. "But I do know what she *is* doing and that is not helping."

"I think it's partly Danielle's fault," I said. "Mary-Kate acts different when she's around. And her mother's the one who gave Mary-Kate that nickname."

"Hey—check it out," Brittany said, nodding toward the parking lot.

A white Mercedes convertible pulled into the Click parking lot, driven by a woman wearing a scarf and sunglasses. We all recognized it—Diana Donovan's car. And Danielle was sitting in the backseat.

"Why isn't Danielle in the front next to Diana?" Lauren asked.

"Yeah," Brittany said. "That's weird."

The car stopped, and Danielle said something

to Diana. Then Diana put the car into reverse and turned around.

"Hey," Brittany said. "Who's that in the front passenger seat? See that blond hair? Someone's ducking down in the seat."

I stared. The blond head popped up for a quick second and then ducked down again.

But a second was all I needed to recognize my own sister.

"It's Mary-Kate!" Lauren gasped. "It looks like . . . Is she hiding from us?"

The car pulled out of the lot and drove away. "What was that all about?" I wondered.

"That was so weird," Lauren said.

"I don't believe it," Brittany said. "Mary-Kate isn't working on the play. She's hanging out with Diana and Danielle again! That's the second time she's blown us off to be with them."

"The second time we know about," Lauren corrected Brittany.

"And she didn't want us to see her," I said, still stunned.

"What do you think she's up to?" Lauren asked.

"Probably sneaking off to see Matt Cader or some other movie star," Brittany joked, naming a hot young actor. "At his secret Hollywood hideaway."

"Yeah," Lauren added. "But no one can see her, or it will be all over the tabloids!"

"That's why she has to wear sunglasses all the time now," Brittany said. "So no one will recognize the big star!"

I laughed along with them, but inside I was hurt. Mary-Kate had never hidden from me before. What was she trying to keep from me?

chapter ten

"Miss Donovan! Miss Donovan!"

"Miss Donovan! Over here!"

I blinked as another camera flashed in my face. The opening of *Sweet Marie* was mobbed with photographers, reporters, and fans. Diana, Danielle, and I were surrounded as soon as we stepped out of the limousine. Diana beamed and led us through the crowd.

"Smile, darling," Diana whispered to me. "Your picture will probably be in the paper tomorrow!"

She didn't need to tell me to smile—I was having a blast. My beautiful blue Carucci dress sparkled in the glare of the flashbulbs. Diana looked fantastic in a simple but clingy red dress, and Danielle wore a pale green vintage gown.

"Miss Donovan! Can we talk to you for a minute?"

I marched down the red carpet next to Diana. Danielle fell behind, slouching. I couldn't stop staring at the celebrities all around us. There was an actor from one of my favorite TV shows with his movie-star girlfriend. There were Cleo Raymond and Colin Davies from Diana's movie, holding hands. *I guess they're not a secret anymore*, I thought.

As we got near the entrance of the movie theater, Diana decided to stop and talk to a reporter from *Celebrity Today*.

"Diana, how long have you been a blonde?" the reporter asked.

Diana patted her hair and asked, "Do you like it, darling? It's for the film I just finished shooting, *Killer Boyfriend*. But I think I might stay blond for a while. You know what they say. . . ."

"It looks fabulous," the reporter said. "But I love you as a redhead, too."

A burly man wearing an earpiece interrupted them. "Diana, we need you inside, please."

Diana nodded. "Thanks for stopping to talk," the reporter said.

"My pleasure," Diana replied, and we went inside the theater. There were more photographers in the lobby, and several large TV cameras.

"Isn't this fun?" I shouted in Danielle's ear.

"Not especially," she said.

She'd been supercranky from the moment I stepped inside the limo. In fact, she'd been cranky all day.

I was still annoyed with her for demanding that we go to Click that afternoon. Once we pulled into the parking lot and saw Ashley, Brittany, and Lauren sitting out front, she gave in and told Diana to turn around. I felt like an idiot slumped in the front seat, hiding. Diana kept saying, "Mikki darling, what are you doing?"

I didn't bother to explain. She'd never understand. I just hoped Ashley and my friends didn't spot me. If they did, I was dead meat.

But I hadn't seen Ashley since then. When I got home from the photo shoot, she was out with Aaron.

A bell rang and an usher called out, "Please be seated, ladies and gentlemen!"

"Let's go, darlings." Diana started for the theater.

Danielle stopped at the candy counter. "Wait a second. I want some popcorn," she said. Diana sighed as we waited for the guy behind the counter to give Danielle a small bag of popcorn.

"Ready now, love?" Diana asked. Danielle nodded and we went inside the darkened theater.

Diana waved to people she knew as we took our seats. She sat down first, and I sat next to her.

"Move over," Danielle snapped to me. "I'm sitting there."

I moved aside so that Danielle could sit next to her mother. I sat on Danielle's other side. Danielle leaned over to adjust her shoe and spilled popcorn on my lap.

"Whoops. Sorry," she said. But the look on her face made it clear it was no accident.

"Danielle, what's wrong with you?" I whispered. "Are you mad at me?"

"No," she said crisply. "Why would I be mad?"

No matter how many times I asked her about her bad mood, she refused to talk about it. *I give up,* I thought, brushing popcorn off my lap. *I might as well try to enjoy the movie.*

But I wished I had someone to enjoy it with.

I wished Ashley were with me.

I sighed. Ashley and I hadn't spoken to each other much since she caught me with the Carucci shopping bags. I could hardly blame her. I should have kept my shopping date with her and our friends.

And, I had to admit, I'd been neglecting Brittany and Lauren ever since I got back from Vancouver. I was spending more and more time with Diana and Danielle and less time with my real friends. Except when I was bossing them around onstage.

No wonder we hadn't been talking much. They were probably all mad at me. And if they had caught me hiding from them in the front seat of Diana's car . . . they'd be furious.

I'm going to make it up to them, I vowed. *I'll make up for everything—as soon as the play is over.*

The play . . . I couldn't let go of the play. Tyler was coming to see it! What would he think of me?

He'll think I lied to him, I thought. *Even though I didn't exactly lie . . .*

What if I got rid of most of the kids? Then the play wouldn't seem so childish. Did we really need kids playing trees and woodland animals?

I had to do something. The play was only three days away!

❀

"Thank you all for coming to this emergency rehearsal," I said.

I stood on the stage of the Sunshine auditorium addressing the cast and crew of *Snow White*. Mary-Kate hadn't shown up yet and Danielle was late, as usual. I didn't care. It would be a lot easier for me to run the rehearsal without them there.

"As you all know, the grand reopening celebration is only two days away," I said. "Some of us aren't too happy with the sets, but we don't have time to fix them now. We'll just have to live with them as they are."

"Yuck," Darren said, staring at the black, depressing forest.

"It's okay," I went on. "No one will notice the sets, because you all will be so funny and adorable! Everyone had their lines down pretty well until last week, when we kind of got sidetracked . . ."

By a steamroller, I thought, remembering the chaos Mary-Kate caused with her acting lessons. "So let's go over them today. If we can nail them by the end of this rehearsal, we should be fine on Monday night."

Silas, who played the sleepy dwarf, raised his hand. "Do I still have to think about counting sheep during the play?" he asked. "I can't remember what I'm supposed to say."

"No, don't worry about counting sheep," I told him. "Just try to remember your lines." I turned to Hannah and asked, "How are you feeling today?"

"I feel good," she said with her old cheerful smile.

"Not angry at your sister?" I asked. "Not upset about cookies or anything?"

Hannah shook her head.

"Good," I said. "All right, let's start rehearsal."

I was lining up the dwarfs offstage when Mary-Kate ran into the auditorium.

"Sorry I'm late," she said. She pulled a big stack of papers out of her backpack and started handing them out to everybody.

She gave me a stapled sheaf of paper. "What's this?" I asked.

"The new script," Mary-Kate said. "I worked on it all night."

I stared at the title page. *Snow White and the Seven Dwarfs: A Play About Good and Evil.*

What?

"Mikki, I'm sorry, but there's no way everyone can learn new lines now," I protested. "The play is in two days!"

"But I worked so hard on this!" Mary-Kate said. "I stayed up all night and totally rethought the whole play. It really works now."

"Works?" I asked. "What are you talking about? What was wrong with the old script?"

"Read this and you'll see," she said. "I tried to make it more than just a story. It's about the meaning of life!"

I closed my eyes and sighed. The meaning of

life? What had gotten into her? Why did everything have to be big and meaningful all the time? Couldn't anything just be fun?

"Please, Ashley," she said. "The least you can do is read it."

"All right," I agreed. I sat down in the first row and flipped through the script. My heart sank lower and lower with every page.

Mary-Kate had changed *everything*. She had the dwarfs saying ridiculous things the kids would never be able to remember. Like this:

Snow White eats the poisoned apple. She falls to the ground.

HAPPY DWARF: Oh, no! Snow White is dead! It is the Death of Beauty and Goodness! And the Triumph of Evil!

WISE DWARF: Don't be sad. She is not dead, for true Beauty never dies.

I heard giggling nearby as Brittany and Lauren read the script. I would have laughed too if it weren't so depressing.

Then I came to the worst part of all: *Everyone onstage freezes. The Wicked Queen does an interpretive dance. The dance symbolizes all the Evil in the*

105

world coming together to fight against Good. Right in the middle of the play!

That did it. The hair prickled on the back of my neck. It was like electricity before a thunderstorm. I couldn't control my temper any longer.

"A dance?" I shouted. "You stop the action dead in the middle of the play so Danielle can do a dance? About Evil? Are you crazy?"

"Danielle is a great dancer," Mary-Kate said. "I thought it would add a lot to the play."

"We don't need to add anything to the play," I said. "It was fine the way it was. You've done nothing but mess it up!"

"That's what you think!" Mary-Kate said. "People who understand art think differently."

"This isn't about art!" I cried. "It's about you! You've been a bossy pain ever since you got involved with this play!"

"I had to be bossy to make the play better!" Mary-Kate said. "You're just upset because my ideas are better than yours!"

"I am not!" I insisted. "But if that's what you think, why don't you take over the play completely? It's all yours. Make it any way you like. You won't have any help from me."

"Or me," Brittany added.

"Or me, either," Lauren said.

I grabbed my things and walked out. Brittany, Lauren, Ben, and Aaron followed. Mary-Kate was left alone with the children.

Serves her right, I thought. *She thinks she knows what she's doing? Let her do it. She'll see.*

"Where's everybody going?" Darren asked.

I couldn't believe it. Ashley actually walked out on the play! And she took everyone older than four with her—including the hunter, Snow White, and the prince!

That's all right, I told myself. *I'll find a way to pull this off. I'll show her. It will be fantastic!*

"Is Ashley coming back?" Hannah asked.

"Not right now," I said, staring at the fifteen kids seated on the stage in front of me. What was I going to do with them? When would Danielle get here?

Might as well just dig in and get started, I thought. I passed out the scripts. "These are your new lines," I explained.

Silas raised his hand. "Mikki?"

"Yes, Silas."

"I don't know how to read."

I stopped. I'd forgotten that my actors were

only four years old. "Do any of you know how to read?" I asked.

"I can read *The Cat in the Hat*," one girl said.

"How did you learn your lines before?" I asked.

"Ashley told them to us," Darren said. "We practiced them over and over until we remembered them."

I collected the scripts. "All right, we won't be needing these, I guess."

Danielle breezed in, an hour late. *Thank goodness,* I thought. *At last, someone who understands me. She'll help me out.*

"Hey, Danielle," I said. "We've got a little crisis here."

"I'll say." Her lips were pressed together in a straight, angry line.

"What's the matter?" I asked.

She waved a tabloid newspaper in my face. "This!" she cried.

I grabbed the newspaper. It was turned to the gossip page. There was a picture of me at the movie opening the night before, walking down the red carpet with Diana! Danielle was nowhere in sight.

"Hey, it's me!" I exclaimed. "That's so cool!"

"Read the caption," Danielle said.

"Blondes have more fun: Diana Donovan and her

daughter at the opening of Sweet Marie *last night at the Bellagio Theater,"* I read out loud.

Uh-oh. No wonder Danielle was upset.

"It's just a mistake," I said. "I can't help it if the photographer got it wrong."

"You were in *my* place," Danielle said. "*I* should have been standing next to Diana. She's *my* mother! And it's *my* life, not yours! So why don't you just stay out of it!"

"Danielle, I never meant to take your place!" I said.

"Leave me alone!" she cried. "I don't want to see you anymore. Find another Wicked Queen! I quit!"

She stormed out of the room, slamming the door behind her. It echoed through the empty auditorium.

"Mikki, why is everybody yelling at you today?" Darren asked.

I rubbed my forehead. I felt a headache coming on—a bad one.

"I don't know, Darren," I said. "I guess it's just not my day."

"Are we still doing the play?" Hannah asked.

What choice did I have? All their parents—and about a hundred other people—were coming on Monday night, expecting to see *Snow White*. I'd just have to do it all myself.

"Yes," I told them. "We're still doing the play. But we need a new Snow White, a new prince, a new hunter and a new Wicked Queen. Anybody want to volunteer?"

The kids just blinked at me.

"You're in big trouble," Darren said.

I sighed and shook my head. "I know it."

chapter eleven

"Give me a whipped mochaccino, Malcolm," I ordered as I settled at the counter at Click. I'd gone there after rehearsal, hoping to find Ashley and the others. But the only person I knew at the café was Malcolm, and he was working.

I have no idea where all my friends are, I realized with a start. That never would have happened before—before I went to Vancouver. Before I came home and ruined everything.

I want everything to be like that again, I thought. *How can I make things go back to the way they were before?*

"Better make it a double," I told Malcolm. "With extra whipped cream." Enough iced green tea.

"Tough day?" Malcolm asked.

He had no idea.

"I just came from a rehearsal for *Snow White*," I told him. "Everybody quit the play except for me and the four-year-olds."

"Yeah, I heard you've been a real pain in the butt lately," Malcolm said.

Leave it to Malcolm to be Mr. Tactful.

"It was exhausting!" I complained. "I never realized how hard Ashley worked to keep the kids in line. They're so spacey! They wander off if you don't watch them, and I don't know how she ever got them to remember their lines. . . ."

And the new sets looked horrible, I thought. And the lighting makes the kids look like monsters. . . . The whole thing was a complete mess.

"Sounds rough," Malcolm said. "You couldn't pay me to do a play with four-year-olds. Not for a million dollars. But that's just me."

"They're really cute, though," I said. I sighed. Who was I kidding?

I dropped my head on the counter.

"Oh, Malcolm," I wailed. "I have so many problems! I have no friends left—not even Danielle! She's mad because there was a picture in the paper of Diana and her daughter—only it showed me, not Danielle! And this guy I like is coming to town today and he wants to see the play! He thinks it's some kind of arty experimental theater piece—he has no idea it's for a day-care center. And even for a kiddie play, it's terrible! And when he sees it he's going to think I'm a moron!"

"There, there," Malcolm said with no sympathy at all. "Here's your coffee, Mary-Kate." He set the cup in front of me.

"It's Mikki now," I told him, lifting my head.

He snorted. "I'm not calling anybody Mikki. It's a stupid name, even for a boy. I won't even call Mickey Mouse Mickey. I call him Mick Mouse. Sounds cooler."

I laughed and reached for my coffee. "Call me whatever you want," I said. "I don't care anymore."

"That's the spirit," Malcolm said.

Where is Ashley? I wondered. I went home after Click, hoping to find her there, but Mom said she was still out. I lay on my bed in my room, wishing she'd come home. I wanted to talk to her and straighten a few things out.

The phone rang. *Maybe that's her,* I thought. But when I answered it, I heard a guy's voice on the other end.

"Mikki? It's Tyler."

"Tyler!" I said. It was good to hear his voice.

113

"How are you? Where are you calling from?"

"Great. I just got into town about an hour ago. Listen, are you busy tonight? I was wondering if you wanted to get together for dinner."

"No, I'm not busy," I said. If he only knew. He was the only person on earth who wanted to hang out with me! "Dinner sounds good."

"Excellent. Where should we meet?"

I picked a café near the beach and told him to meet me there. Then I thought about what to wear. What kind of clothes would impress a guy like Tyler?

I scanned my closet, thinking, *Glamorous? Artsy? Intellectual?*

My head began to spin, and I sat on my bed. It took so much energy trying to be someone I wasn't. All of a sudden I just felt tired.

I picked out a pair of jeans and a top. There was no use in pretending with Tyler anymore. He'd find out the truth soon enough.

I pulled up in front of the café an hour later. Tyler was waiting for me at a table on the terrace.

"It's great to see you again, Mikster." He stood up and kissed me on the cheek.

"You, too, Tyler," I said. "Welcome to Los Angeles."

The waiter brought menus and we ordered something to drink. I could feel Tyler staring at me as I read the menu.

"Are you all right?" he asked.

"Sure," I replied. "Why?"

"You look different than you did in Vancouver," he said. "Kind of frazzled. Are you having problems with the play? I bet directing can be a real headache."

"Actually, I am having problems," I admitted, and before I knew it, it was all pouring out of me.

"First of all, I have to tell you something," I said. "The play I'm doing isn't some kind of arty experimental theater piece. It's a day-care-center play starring my friends and a bunch of four-year-olds."

Tyler started laughing. I just kept going. I wanted to get it all out before I lost my nerve. Then he could think whatever he wanted about me. It was out of my hands.

"I tried so hard to make the play something special," I said. "But I ended up ruining the whole thing! I was such a jerk. I forgot that the play wasn't supposed to be about me showing off how smart I am. It's for the kids and their parents. It's supposed to be fun! But it's too late now. The play is a mess

115

and all my friends are mad at me—even my sister, Ashley! So don't bother coming on Monday night—it's going to be a disaster."

Tyler was laughing harder than ever now.

That's it, I thought. *He's not going to want to hang with me anymore now that he knows the truth. Now that he knows I'm an obnoxious jerk and I'm not nearly as glamorous or artsy as I pretended to be. Now that he knows Mikki was just a mask. Now that he sees the real Mary-Kate.*

He stopped laughing and sipped his drink. "I can't wait to see the play," he finally said. "I think it's so cute that you're working with little kids. I don't like pretentious plays. What made you think I did?"

"I don't know," I said. "I just assumed—"

He reached across the table and put his hand over mine. "Mikki, you don't have to impress me. I already like you."

Hmmm. Blurting out the truth was working out pretty well. Why stop now?

"That's another thing," I said. "My name isn't Mikki. It's Mary-Kate. And I like bowling, even though it's so three-years-ago, and I like Rave, and cheesy boy bands, and diet soda, and ice cream floats. . . ."

116

Tyler was laughing again.

"And I'm not nearly as in or fabulous as I pretended to be on the movie set," I continued. "I just wanted to fit in with you and Danielle and Cleo and everybody so badly—"

"Mary-Kate," he said. "I like your real name better than Mikki. And I like you—the real you. You didn't have to lie to me."

Wow. I was starting to feel a lot better. I took a deep breath. *Welcome back, Mary-Kate.* It was good to relax and be myself again.

But I still had a problem—a big one.

"The play," I said. "I messed up the sets and the lighting, and the kids are all confused now and don't know their lines. . . . And three of my main actors quit on me! What am I going to do?"

"We still have a day to work on it," Tyler said. We? I liked that. "Maybe I can help you."

"Thanks," I said. "But how can we ever fix everything in one day? It's impossible!"

"We'll see," he said.

chapter twelve

"What's this?" I asked. I came home from an afternoon of shopping with Mom to find a note on my bed. It said,

> Dear Ashley,
> Please come to the day-care center sometime after four today. It's very important.
>
> Love,
> Mary-Kate

My first thought was that I wasn't going anywhere near the day-care center again. It was too much of a headache. Mary-Kate wanted to be in charge, so let her. I wanted nothing more to do with the play.

But then I reread the note. Hmmm, I thought. She

signed it "Mary-Kate." Why not Mikki? I wondered.

It was a good sign, and I was interested. Mikki got on my nerves, but I missed Mary-Kate. Still, I tried not to get my hopes up. Mary-Kate was probably freaking out about the play and just wanted me to help her.

Well, I won't, I vowed. No matter how much she begs me to!

I got in the car and headed for the center. When I reached the auditorium, I found Mary-Kate in the middle of a rehearsal with the kids. She didn't see me come in. I sat down in the back and watched.

The lighting was different, I noticed. Much better. And the sets—someone had painted the trees green again! The forest looked beautiful!

"Okay, kids, get ready," Mary-Kate said. "Here's the part where you find Snow White!"

A very cute guy I'd never seen before stepped onstage with a sweater wrapped around his waist like a skirt. Mary-Kate and the children laughed when they saw him.

He lay down on a cot and pretended to be asleep. The seven dwarfs marched into the house.

"Look! Our house is all clean!" Darren said.

"Somebody cleaned it up for us!" Silas said sleepily.

"I liked it better dirty!" Hannah said grouchily.

The kids were doing great! They were getting their lines right. And it looked like they were relaxed and having fun.

"Achoo!" said the sneezy dwarf. "Look! Someone is sleeping in our bed!"

The dwarfs surrounded the sleeping guy. He opened his eyes, sat up, and screamed. "Oh, my!" he cried in a high-pitched, girly voice. "Who are you?"

The kids laughed again.

"We're the Seven Dwarfs," Darren said. "Who are you?"

"Why, I'm Snow White," the guy said.

"That's a boy," Hannah said. "He's not Snow White!"

Uh-oh, I thought. Hannah's out of character again. Here comes the lecture about cookies from Mary-Kate.

But Mary-Kate just laughed. "You're all doing great," she told the kids. "Let's keep going."

I walked up to the stage. "Hi, Mary-Kate," I said.

"Ashley!" She shielded her eyes from the stage lights so she could see me. "You came!"

"What's going on here?" I asked.

"Let's take a quick break, okay, kids?" Mary-

Kate said. She beckoned to "Snow White" and met me at the front of the stage.

"This is Tyler McGuire," she said. "Tyler, this is Ashley."

"Hi, Ashley," Tyler said. So that was Tyler. Wow—he was great-looking.

"Tyler helped me redo the sets and the lighting," Mary-Kate said. "And he's got two little sisters at home, so he's great with kids. We've been rehearsing all afternoon, and the kids have almost got it down perfectly!"

"That's great!" I said. "I saw some of it, and it looked really good."

"Oh, Snow White," Darren called. "You dropped your skirt!" He waved Tyler's sweater.

"You give that back!" Tyler teased in his girly voice. He chased after Darren, who burst into giggles.

"Looks like the kids are having fun," I said.

Mary-Kate nodded. "I finally realized that was the whole point of the play. I'm sorry I was such a jerk, Ashley. I was so caught up in making the play what I wanted, I forgot it was really for the kids."

"That's okay," I said.

"No, it isn't," she said. "I was so into being Mikki that I gave up all the things I really love! Like ice cream floats, and spending time with my friends, and talking things over with my best friend—you. Can you ever forgive me, Ashley?"

"Hmmm," I said. "Let me think about this a minute. Are you saying we can do this play *my* way? And you won't butt in at all?"

Mary-Kate nodded. "I promise. But there is one change. It looks like I'll have to play the Wicked Queen after all. Danielle is mad at me, just like everybody else. I called her this morning to apologize, but she hasn't called me back."

"Hold it right there, Mikki," a voice called from the back. "You won't get away with this!"

I stared through the glare of the stage lights. Danielle!

chapter thirteen

"**N**obody steals a part from Danielle Bloom!" Danielle shouted. She marched up to the stage. "I got your message and came right over. I was born to play the Wicked Queen!"

"That's for sure," Ashley whispered to me.

"Shhh!" I scolded her, giggling.

Danielle didn't hear her, luckily. "Are you sure you want to come back to the play?" I asked her. "What about the picture in the newspaper and everything?"

"I'm sorry about the way I acted," Danielle said. "I freaked over that photo—"

"I totally understand," I said. "If I saw a picture of you in the paper and the caption said it was me, I'd be upset, too."

"Maybe so, but you were right," Danielle went

on. "It wasn't your fault the photographer made a mistake. I can see why people thought you were Diana's daughter—her hair is practically the same color as yours now."

"But I should have let you walk down the red carpet next to her," I said. "I was so stunned by all the lights and the people, I wasn't thinking. . . ."

"That wasn't your fault either," Danielle said. "Diana wanted you next to her." She paused. "She's been paying a lot of attention to you lately, and I was jealous," she admitted. "That's why I haven't been so friendly to you."

"I was hanging around with you guys an awful lot," I said. "It was just so exciting for me. . . . But I'm sorry about that. I should have been more sensitive to how you felt about it. Instead I got all caught up in the shopping and opening and the cast party. . . ."

"Don't worry about it, Mikki," Danielle said. "Diana and I had a talk last night. She *wanted* you around because you look up to her. And she thinks I don't. But I do . . . so we're working things out. Trying to communicate better."

"That's great," I said. "By the way, I'm not going by Mikki anymore. I'm back to plain old Mary-Kate."

"Really?" Danielle raised an eyebrow. "Okay, cool, Mary-Kate. I think everything's going to be fine." Then she smushed up her face to make it look witchy.

"Just fine, my pretty," she said in a wicked voice. She cupped her hand and pretended to offer me a make-believe apple. "As long as you take a bite of this sweet, juicy apple!"

I laughed. "All right!" I called out. "Everybody, the Wicked Queen is back!"

"Hooray!" the kids cheered.

Things were falling into place. But I still needed someone to play the hunter and Snow White. If only I could convince Brittany and Lauren that Mikki was gone and Mary-Kate was back!

chapter fourteen

"The place is packed!" I said to Tyler.

"Yeah," Tyler agreed. "I think you've got a hit on your hands!"

We were standing in the back of the Sunshine Day Care Center auditorium, waiting for *Snow White* to start.

The stage lights came on and the play began. The seven dwarfs marched onto the stage, looking adorable. The audience *ooohed* and *ahhhed*.

Next, Danielle chewed up the scenery as the Wicked Queen. Brittany and Lauren had agreed to come back, and they were both perfect in their roles.

"This is really terrific," Tyler said. "The sets look great and the kids are fantastic!"

"Thanks," I said.

When the play ended, the audience rose to its feet for a standing ovation. The little kids glowed. Then Lauren brought Ashley out to take a bow.

"We couldn't have done it without our brilliant director, Ashley Olsen!" Lauren exclaimed.

Ashley grinned and took a bow with the rest of the cast. I clapped so hard, my hands stung. I was so proud of all of them!

Diana kissed Danielle. "You were fantastic as always, darling," Diana said. Danielle smiled. It was great to see them getting along for a change.

Mom and Dad rushed up and hugged Ashley and me. "Congratulations, girls!" Dad said. "The play was a big success!"

"Thank you so much for all your hard work," Mom added. "You really made our reopening celebration special."

"Why don't we all go to Big Jonesy's to celebrate?" Dad suggested.

"I've heard of that place," Tyler said. "It's an old diner from the fifties, right? I'd love to go there."

Ashley glanced at me. "Are you up for that?"

"Definitely," I said. "Being Mikki and hanging out with celebrities is fine, but being Mary-Kate is fabulous enough for me! And anyway, I'm dying for a vanilla root beer float!"

Find out what happens next in

Book 10:
Keeping Secrets

"Where were you last night?" I asked my friend Brittany as we headed to the cafeteria. "I thought you were going to meet me and Mary-Kate at Click."

"Take a wild guess, Ashley," Brittany said, rolling her eyes.

"Baby-sitting for Lucas again, huh?" I said.

"Mom and Dad don't even bother to ask anymore if I can baby-sit," Brittany complained. "They just announce they're leaving and the next thing I hear is the door slamming." She stopped at her locker, twirled in her combination, and swung open the door.

"It sounds like you need to talk to your parents," I said. I understood Brittany's frustration. I wouldn't want to be a full-time, on-call baby-sitter either—even though Lucas is the cutest baby in the world.

I glanced down the hallway. A group of cheerleaders laughed as Bill, a guy I knew from English class, passed by. I thought I heard one of them say something about his girlfriend two-timing him.

"Britt, did you hear that?" I asked. "What is going on today? Everyone's talking about each other."

"I know what you mean," Brittany said. She shut her locker and we continued down the hall. "It's like gossip central around here!"

"I need to make a quick pit-stop in the bathroom." I led the way into the girl's room. The smell of powder, deodorant, and mold hit my nose. I spotted an empty stall and slipped inside.

The bathroom door opened and slammed shut. "Yeah, I heard that, too," a girl said. I didn't recognize her voice. "Aaron definitely wants to break up with his girlfriend."

I froze. *Were they talking about* my *boyfriend, Aaron?*

ENTER TO WIN
TWO NEW FRAGRANCES FROM

the **mary-kateandashley** brand

100
Grand Prize Winners

**will win a
set of 2 Fragrances:
mary-kateandashley one
and
mary-kateandashley two**

MARY-KATE AND ASHLEY SWEET 16
Fragrance Sweepstakes

OFFICIAL RULES:

1. No purchase necessary.

2. To enter complete the official entry form or hand print your name, address, age, and phone number along with the words "MARY-KATE AND ASHLEY SWEET 16 Fragrance Sweepstakes" on a 3" x 5" card and mail to: MARY-KATE AND ASHLEY SWEET 16 Fragrance Sweepstakes, c/o HarperEntertainment, Attn: Children's Marketing Department, 10 East 53rd Street, New York, NY 10022. Entries must be received by September 30, 2003. Enter as often as you wish, but each entry must be mailed separately. One entry per envelope. Partially completed, illegible, or mechanically reproduced entries will not be accepted. Sponsors are not responsible for lost, late, mutilated, illegible, stolen, postage due, incomplete, or misdirected entries. All entries become the property of Dualstar Entertainment Group, LLC, and will not be returned.

3. Sweepstakes open to all legal residents of the United States (excluding Colorado and Rhode Island), who are between the ages of five and fifteen on September 30, 2003, excluding employees and immediate family members of HarperCollins Publishers, Inc., ("HarperCollins"), Parachute Properties and Parachute Press, Inc., and their respective subsidiaries and affiliates, officers, directors, shareholders, employees, agents, attorneys, and other representatives (individually and collectively "Parachute"), Dualstar Entertainment Group, LLC, and its subsidiaries and affiliates, officers, directors, shareholders, employees, agents, attorneys, and other representatives (individually and collectively "Dualstar"), and their respective parent companies, affiliates, subsidiaries, advertising, promotion and fulfillment agencies, and the persons with whom each of the above are domiciled. Offer void where prohibited or restricted by law.

4. Odds of winning depend on the total number of entries received. Approximately 300,000 sweepstakes announcements published. All prizes will be awarded. Winners will be randomly drawn on or about October 15, 2003, by HarperCollins, whose decisions are final. Potential winner will be notified by mail and will be required to sign and return an affidavit of eligibility and release of liability within 14 days of notification. Prizes won by minors will be awarded to parent or legal guardian who must sign and return all required legal documents. By acceptance of the prize, winner consents to the use of his or her name, photograph, likeness, and biographical information by HarperCollins, Parachute, Dualstar, and for publicity purposes without further compensation except where prohibited.

5. One hundred (100) Grand Prize Winners each win a set of two fragrances: *mary-kateandashley one* and *mary-kateandashley two*. Approximate retail value of each prize: $12.87.

6. Only one prize will be awarded per individual, family, or household. Prizes are non-transferable and cannot be substituted, sold or redeemed for cash. Any federal, state, or local taxes are the responsibility of the winner. Sponsor may substitute prize of equal or greater value, if necessary, at its sole discretion.

7. Additional terms: By participating, entrants agree a) to the official rules and decisions of the judges, which will be final in all respects; and to waive any claim to ambiguity of the official rules and b) to release, discharge, and hold harmless HarperCollins, Parachute, Dualstar, and their respective parent companies, affiliates, subsidiaries, advertising, promotion and fulfillment agencies from and against any and all liability or damages associated with acceptance, use, or misuse of any prize received in this sweepstakes.

8. Any dispute arising from this Sweepstakes will be determined according to the laws of the State of New York, without reference to its conflict of law principles, and the entrants consent to the personal jurisdiction of the State and Federal courts located in New York County and agree that such courts have exclusive jurisdiction over all such disputes.

9. To obtain the name of the winners, please send your request and a self-addressed stamped envelope (residents of Vermont may omit return postage) to MARY-KATE AND ASHLEY SWEET 16 Fragrance Sweepstakes Winners, c/o HarperEntertainment, Attn: Children's Marketing Department, 10 East 53rd Street, New York, NY 10022 by November 1, 2003. Sweepstakes Sponsor: HarperCollins Publishers, Inc.

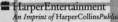